NAR

ADVANCE PRAISE

A vividly described journey into the life of a historical woman revered as a goddess, Monica Gupta creates a world of rich detail that one can sink into. With the character of Narayani, she gives us a new heroine for our times; for all times.

—**Kiran Manral**
Author

This is a wonderfully woven tale of courage, pathos, and a spirit of resistance told with much empathy and vividity that will engage the reader. Some passages jump out for their empathy and emotional connect with the reader, while others for the veer rasa they portray.

—**Abhinav Agarwal**
Chief Curator, Indica Books

Narayani: True Story of a Sati is an interesting narrative of a folk goddess in modern-day Rajasthan and Haryana. The narrative has some touching moments of reality which the reader, especially the womenfolk of our country will empathize with. Beautiful and real-life narration will have the reader glued to the book till the end.

—**Utkarsh Patel**
Faculty, Comparative Mythology

It's a beautiful book that harps on the culture and sentiments of a time when patriarchy ruled. But with the emergence of Narayani that patriarchy is challenged. The depiction is balanced, powerful, and fluid.

—**Amrita Mukherjee**
Author and Journalist

There are so many women who have built the pages of history but got lost in translations. Monica writes about one such woman, who we know today as a Goddess and deity. Monica makes Narayani's story relatable, inspiring, and aspirational and enables one to dream of achieving such Goddess-like qualities. She brings to life the reasons why Narayani became timeless and is still worshipped far and wide. To do justice to a story like this is not easy, but Monica's simplicity of writing and the intention of why she chose to tell this story validates her as a writer of superior talent. I lived the story through her characters and hope all readers do too. The story of the evolution of the women of India, the growth of India as a country, and an interesting account of the very roots of our culture are what *Narayani: True Story of a Sati* is about.

—Shaina Shah
Film Maker and Actor

I loved reading *Narayani: True Story of a Sati*!
It took me into an untold era of history and showed me stereotypes as well as progressive mindsets of people like Narayani's father. The story keeps you hooked from the very beginning and takes you along with the life and adventures of Narayani. Narayani emerges as the epitome of true women empowerment. Written in a lucid way, the author leaves you wanting more at every stage of the story! It's a must-read and a book that you would want to keep in your personal library.

—Dr Falguni Vasavada
Prof of Marketing, MICA

MEMBER

· Standing Committee Human Resource Development
· Consultative Committee Urban Development
· Parliamentary Committee on Official Language
· Committee - Welfare of Other Backward Classes
· Hindi Salahkar Samiti - Micro, Small & Medium Enterprises
· Joint Committee - Right to Fair Compensation and Transparancy in Land Acquisition,
  Rehabititation and Resetilement (Second Amendment Bill, 2015)

सत्यमेव जयते

Santosh Ahlawat
Member of Parliament
(Lok Sabha)
Jhunjhunu (Rajasthan)

निमितः–

श्रीमती मोनिका सुधीर गुप्ता
अहमदाबाद (गुजरात)।

महोदया,

    आपको बधाई देते हुए मन को प्रसन्नता हो रही है कि एक प्रेरणादायी पुस्तक ''नारायणी—एक सच्ची कहानी'' आपने लिखी है। इससे आगामी पीढ़ी को हमारे इतिहास व धार्मिक आस्थाओं के बारे में तथ्यो की सही जानकारी होगी और साथ ही एक महिला जो कि शक्ति रूपा देवी होती है, उसकी क्षमताओं, त्याग तथा तपस्या की पवित्र भावनाओं के बारे में भी भावी पीढ़ी को जानकारी होगी।

    मै आपकी इस पुस्तक के सफल प्रकाशन की शुभकामना प्रकट करती हूँ।

भवदीय,

(संतोष अहलावत)

पूर्व सांसद झुन्झुनू, पुर्व विधायक सूरजगढ, प्रदेश उपाध्यक्ष भाजपा राजस्थान

जे. पी. चन्देलिया
पूर्व आई.ए.एस.
विधायक, पिलानी (राज.)
सभापति
राजस्थान विधानसभा-विशेषाधिकार समिति

81/ B-101, अरावली एनक्लेव
न्यू सांगानेर रोड़, मानसरोवर
जयपुर-302020
ईमेल:-mlapilani2018@gmail.com
मो.: 9414085388

No. MLA PILANI 2018/2023-24/4650   Date:- 13-07-2023

श्रीमती मोनिका सुधीर गुप्ता
अहमदाबाद (गुजरात)।

महोदया,

आपको बधाई देते हुए मन को प्रसन्नता हो रही है कि एक प्रेरणादायी पुस्तक "नारायणी—एक   सच्ची कहानी" आपने लिखी है। इससे आगामी पीढ़ी को हमारे इतिहास व धार्मिक आस्थाओं के बारे में तथ्यों की सही जानकारी होगी और साथ ही एक महिला जो कि शक्ति रूपा देवी होती है, उसकी क्षमताओं, त्याग तथा तपस्या की पवित्र भावनाओं के बारे में भी भावी पीढ़ी को जानकारी होगी।

मै आपकी इस पुस्तक के सफल प्रकाशन की शुभकामना प्रकट करता हूँ।

सादर

भवदीय,

(जे.पी. चन्देलिया)
विधायक, पिलानी

श्रीमती मोनिका सुधीर गुप्ता जी,

आपकी पुस्तक नारायणी "एक सती की सच्ची कहानी" के विषय में जितनी प्रशंसा की जाए वह कम ही होगी। कारण, यह कि आपने विषय ही ऐसा चुना है जो समस्त संसार के हृदय में पहले से ही अंकित है। आपने तो पुज्य नारायणी दादी के चरित्र को काफी विस्तार से उजागर करते हुए भारतीय नारी के त्याग, उसकी तपस्या, समर्पण और उसकी दैवीय शक्तियों को इतने अधिक प्रभावी स्वरूप से उजागर किया है कि लगता है यह सभी घटनाएं हमारी नजरो के समक्ष साक्षात घटित हो रही हैं। इसके अलावा मौजुदा समय की प्रबल मांग के अनुसार आपने हिन्दु धर्म को लेकर जिस आस्था के दर्शन अपनी पुस्तक में कराए हैं वह अविस्मरणीय है। हम यथार्थ के धरातल से जुड़े आपके इस प्रयास की मुक्त कंठ से सराहना करते है। निश्चित रूप से यह पुस्तक भारतीय नारी को अपने भीतर छिपी शक्तियों को उजागर करने में मददगार होगी साथ ही आज की युवा पीढ़ी को हिन्दु धर्म के प्रति जागरूक करने में सफल होगी। आपको ठेरों शुभकामनाएं।

मंत्री   _Skrishna Rana_

श्री सतीधाम सेवा समिति
दिल्ली चकला, अहमदवाद

श्रीमती मोनिका   03 अगस्त 2023
सुधीर गुप्ता जी
(अध्यक्ष अहमदाबाद बुक क्लब)

विषय :- नारायणी - एक सती की सच्ची कहानी पुस्तक "मिल के पत्थर" समान

महोदया, सादर जय दादी की।

आपके द्वारा लिखित पुस्तक " नारायणी - एक सती की सच्ची कहानी " के विषय में जितनी भी प्रशंसा की जाए वह कम ही होगी। कारण, यह कि आपने विषय ही ऐसा चुना है जो समस्त संसार के हृदय में पहले से ही अंकित है। आपने तो पूज्य नारायणी दादी के चरित्र को काफी विस्तार से उजागर करते हुए भारतीय नारी के त्याग, उसकी तपस्या, समर्पण और उसकी दैवीय शक्तियों को इतने अधिक प्रभावी स्वरूप से उजागर किया है कि लगता है यह सभी घटनाएं हमारी नज़रों के समक्ष साक्षात घटित हो रही हैं। इसके अलावा मौजूदा समय की प्रबल मांग के अनुरूप आपने हिन्दू धर्म को लेकर जिस आस्था के दर्शन अपनी पुस्तक में कराए हैं वह अविस्मरणीय है। हम यथार्थ के धरातल से जुड़े आपके इस प्रयास की मुक्त कंठ से सराहना करते हैं। निश्चित रूप से यह पुस्तक भारतीय नारी को अपने भीतर छिपी शक्तियों को उजागर करने में मददगार होगी साथ ही आज की युवा पीढ़ी को हिन्दू धर्म के प्रति जागरूक करने में भी सफल होगी। आपको ढेरों शुभकामनाएं।

संजय टिबड़ेवाल   अश्विन गुप्ता

अध्यक्ष   मंत्री

श्री राणी शक्ति सेवा समिति शाहीबाग अहमदाबाद

NARAYANI
True story of a Sati

Monica Sudhir Gupta

Vitasta

Published by
Renu Kaul Verma
Vitasta Publishing Pvt Ltd
2/15, Ansari Road, Daryaganj
New Delhi - 110 002
info@vitastapublishing.com

ISBN: 978-81-19670-02-4
© Monica Sudhir Gupta
First Edition 2023
MRP ₹395

Edited by Anuradha Mukherjee
Typeset & Cover Design by Somesh Kumar Mishra
Printed by Vikas Computer and Printers, New Delhi

To
Rani Sati Dadi

सर्वमङ्गलमाङ्गल्ये शिवे सर्वार्थसाधिके ।
शरण्ये त्र्यम्बके गौरि नारायणि नमोऽस्तु ते ॥

Contents

Preface

This record of Narayani's life came about serendipitously; almost like divine intervention.

In 2019, during my visit to the Rani Sati temple in Jhunjhunu, I was performing the 108 *pheres* around the sanctum while chanting the Narayani Chalisa when I heard my conscious mind ask, *Who is she? What is her story? What makes her godly? Do you know?*

Although I had worshipped Rani Sati Dadi since my childhood, I had no answers except that she was our *kuldev*i, she had committed Sati, and she was Uttara's reincarnation. This certainly didn't satisfy my mind. I wanted to know more. This was my divine call—to know Narayani, the girl who became Rani Sati Dadi. Except for a few facts, the web didn't have too much information available.

I picked up the *Narayani Charit Manas* from a bookstore nearby, but I struggled to read and understand the Hindi poetic verses in it. I was instantly reminded of Tony Morrison's words, 'If you find a book you really want to read but it hasn't been written yet, then you must write it'. I was reminded of Luv and Kush. Had they not sung the Ramayana, would the Ayodhyawasis have realised their fault? Would Ram know the truth? Would the world know of the Ramayana and its characters? Probably not!

I immediately got down to my research with a conviction to tell the world Narayani's story; the becoming of Rani Sati Dadi. As I belonged to the same community that worships her, the elderly were my main source of information. When I spoke to the present and future generations, they only had the broad facts, not the nuances that made up the inspirational parts. I decided to write for these future and contemporary readers. To bring the story out from the temples and share it internationally. To do so, I realigned my perspective of her. I started seeing Narayani as a human and decided I had to write a modern-day retelling of her story.

Her specific date of birth hasn't been documented, but she lived during the medieval period, between the thirteenth and fifteenth centuries. After reading extensively about the Mughal invasion era and the geographical factors of the area, and gathering stories from various devotees, my framework was ready. In this entire three-year research process, I inferred that Narayani was not just a religious figure but a historical hero. Throughout her extraordinarily lived life, she broke out of the hackneyed roles set for women by society and redefined their identities to meet the challenges of the period. She inspired girls to realise their harnessed powers and make them purposeful. Her parenting by a feminist father taught other parents the importance of education and self-defense. Her sacrifice to avenge her husband's death taught people how to live a life of honour. She was the epitome of a Kalyug woman, reincarnated from the Dwapara Yuga to have her wish fulfilled and set new norms for women. She was destined to be a modern female warrior.

Acknowledgment

My MOST SINCERE THANKS to my family, friends, well-wishers, readers, and all those who have generously provided their support, encouragement, and blessings throughout the creation of the Narayani story. My Publisher, Renu Kaul Verma, and the entire Vitasta family for having faith in me and bringing out the best version of this book. You all are the best!

Sudarshan Gupta, my father-in-law for his constant support in connecting me with the right people for research. Thank you, Papa!

Tina Singh, my first reader of the rough draft. Your timely assurance was helpful. Thanks, Tina!

Rachna Gupta. Your reviews are always insightful!

Authors whose books were helpful resources:
- Shri Ramakant Sharma, *Narayani Charit Manas*.
- Shri Hargovind Murarkar, *Shri Rani Sati Dadiji ki Amarkatha*.

Sudha Gupta, my mother for instilling in me a love for books, and teaching me the power of words.

Thank you, Sudhir Gupta, Anant, and Vivaan for being my backbone.

Most importantly, my revered thank you to Rani Sati Dadi for choosing me to write your story!

Prologue

With a shawl wrapped around him, he sat hunched over, his face full of lines drawn by wisdom and memories. Ranaji, an octogenarian now, stood up with tremendous effort. Holding a *lathi* in his left hand, he pushed open the huge wooden door. He then walked towards the platform in the middle of the compound. With trembling hands, he lifted the corner of his shawl and wiped the trident that stood on the platform. As the dust cleared, the first rays of the morning sun entered Shakti Dham and fell on the trident as if paying their reverence and then scattered to light up the world. Ranaji sat down beside it with a great sigh, a distant look in his eyes.

His reverie was broken by a gentle touch on his feet. He looked up at the two little faces standing before him.

'Ranaji, I am Narayani, and this is my twin brother, Narayan', said the girl.

A faint smile broke out on Ranaji's face, making deeper the wrinkles surrounding his jawline and eyes. He looked at the huge crowd assembled in front of him—children, young couples, elderly men and women, strangers from neighbouring states and villages—all looking at him intently.

'Ranaji, we are here with our parents at Shakti Dham to become strong and learned. Bless us, Dadaji!' The children said in unison and sat down beside him.

Ranaji filled their palms with sweet golden *boondi*. Clearing his throat, he spoke, 'And how will you become strong and learned by coming here?'

'I will pray to Rani Shakti Dadi to make me strong', the girl said. 'But I don't understand one thing...why is there no image of her? To whom should I pray? And how? Everyone says that you have met her...tell me, Dadaji, how does a goddess look? Did she have many hands? Was she very beautiful? How are gods born?'

Ranaji looked at the trident. 'Gods are born as humans. It is their choices and actions that make them gods. This *trishul* is Rani Shakti Dadi.'

'But how can a *trishul* be a goddess? It is lifeless. It is not even a girl!' The boy said.

By then, the entire crowd had sat down, eager to hear answers to the questions raised by the kids.

Ranaji ran his fingers over the spikes of the trident. 'She is a goddess not because she was born with supernatural powers or many hands...she is a goddess because she was the chosen one; because she lived an exemplary life and set an example for all of mankind to learn from and follow in this Yug. This *trishul* symbolises the three qualities Lord Vishnu gave her before sending her to this world. The spike in the middle stands for "love", the core of her being; the left one for "conviction", having an indelible faith in oneself; the right one stands for "courage", the strength to grow and change. Her soul travelled many Yugs to have her wish fulfilled, a promise made by Lord Krishna himself, and to fulfil her purpose of enlightening the world about the strength of a woman and how it can be harnessed for the good of an entire society.'

Ranaji looked at the stunned crowd and let out a laugh. 'I know you are confused and have a lot of questions. Let me tell you her story. You will find all your answers then.'

He took a deep breath, 'Rani Shakti Dadi, the epitome of a Kalyug woman, a Devi, symbolised by a *trishul* and believed to be Uttara's reincarnation, was born as Narayani in Dokwa, Haryana, in the twelfth century. This is her story...'

CHAPTER 1

Panchayat Meeting

Gurshamal walked into the house, carrying a cotton bag on his shoulder, sweat from the day's hard work on the back of his grey kurta. Upon hearing his footsteps, Ganga ran into the living room, carrying a *lota* of water and a hand fan.

With a great exhale, Gurshamal dropped his bag on the floor, took off his kurta, and slumped on the charpoy. Ganga sat down beside him and offered him the *lota*. Gurshamal waved it away without uttering a word. Ganga started fanning him.

'The heat has been unbearable today', she said.

'Humph.'

He sat leaning backwards, hands stretched back to rest on the floor and prop up his tired body, eyes closed. Ganga paused momentarily to dab her husband's wet forehead with her *pallu*. A moment's silence later, Gurshamal opened his eyes and reached out for the *lota* in front of him on the floor.

'I had a long day today', he spoke after taking a sip.

'Was it fruitful?'

He shrugged his shoulders before taking another sip. As the water traced a route through his parched throat, he watched the view offered by the ajar door with great intensity—a barren piece of land. Ever since he had migrated to the village of Dokwa along with his wife nearly a decade ago, that patch of land had not changed at all. Over the years, he had seen many farmers tend to it with no success. He had tried his luck too, as a trader of chilli, but in vain. The sight of that peculiar oddity—an arid piece of land amidst lush greenery—always reminded him of his personal anguish and overpowered him with a profound sense of desolation.

As dusk fell rapidly, his grief ran its course, and he turned his attention to matters concerning his trade. While Seth Gurshamal sat down to calculate his profit and loss for the week, Ganga peeled potatoes in the kitchen for dinner.

'Have the chilli prices been increased?' She asked, 'Or is the Panchayat still sleeping over the matter?'

'The administration does not care', said Gurshamal.

Ganga shook her head in quiet dejection. Suddenly, her face lit up as she remembered a recent happy development. Abandoning her half-peeled potatoes, she rushed out of the kitchen.

'You know Lila…she delivered a baby boy last night. I went to see them earlier today. He is so beautiful…just like an angel…I couldn't take my eyes off him the entire time.'

'And how is the mother?'

'She looked a little pale…having two kids in a year's span has drained her health.'

'Hmm.'

Gurshamal and Ganga looked at each other, silently acknowledging each other's thoughts.

'Did you ask?' He spoke finally.

Ganga shook her head. 'I just could not…'

With steps weighed down by the incredible gravity of her thoughts, she had stood outside the house listening to the baby's cries, contemplating whether to go in or not. The box of sweets in her hands had become damp from her sweaty palms. The baby kept crying. Why was no one consoling him? Maybe Lila had gone to the backyard to freshen up. Ganga rushed inside.

The moment she stepped into the house, Lila walked into the room, cradling her baby.

'Oh, it's you', she said, her displeasure no secret.

Ganga put on her most generous smile and said, 'Hello Lila! I was returning from the market when I learnt about the lovely little addition to your family and picked up these sweets for you'.

Lila forced a smile. 'Thank you', she said, extending her hand.

'He resembles his father', Ganga said, handing over the box of sweets.

As she extended her hand to stroke the baby's

head, Lila visibly tightened the grip on her son. Ganga withdrew immediately and said, 'I am so happy for you. I wish I could spend some time with the little one, but I have to leave now…have to cook dinner'.

Recollecting the incident, Ganga dabbed her wet eyes with her pallu. 'How could I ask her for her child?' Touching her womb, she looked across at the barren field, now lit up by the full moon.

'Shall I go and ask?' Gurshamal's words pulled her out of her trance.

'No', she said, swallowing the lump in her throat. 'We have no right to separate a mother from her child. Why should our curse become someone else's?'

Gurshamal looked at her as she hid her face in her hands and sobbed. He tried to find the right words to console her, but he had already said all of them in the years that had gone by. No words could soothe her aching heart. He patted her head gently.

'It's time for our sadhana…', he said.

Ganga calmed down and raised her face, now turned red. 'Oh, yes! I completely forgot…'

Ganga wiped her eyes and rushed into their bedroom. She appeared moments later with two mats tucked under her arms. In front of Lord Narayan's image in their living room, both spread out their mats and sat down cross-legged on them. With their eyes closed, backs straight, arms stretched, and hands resting over their knees, the two meditated in silence. The couple followed this ritual twice every day to invoke positive universal energy to help them remain mindful of their purpose in life and to introspect and reflect upon what they desired and delivered.

Later that night, as Ganga served dinner, she spoke, 'While in sadhana, a thought crossed my mind...by God's grace, we have everything we need. Why don't we express our gratitude to Lord Narayan by conducting a Satyanarayan Katha?'

'What a coincidence you should say that! I have been thinking the same thing...'

'Should we do it next week then?'

'We can do it this week...in fact, we can do it tomorrow.'

'But there isn't enough time to make arrangements!'

'Leave that to me. There should be no delay in God's service.'

The next morning, Gurshamal left home at five in the morning to meet the local pujari, personally invite neighbours and friends, and make other arrangements. In the meantime, Ganga prepared prasad for the puja and decorated the house with lanterns and flowers. Although they had very little time, the couple made sure that every detail, big and small, was tended to with care and devotion.

It was around six in the evening when the couple finally saw the last of their guests leave. Exhausted yet elevated in their spirits, the two sat down for their evening ritual. Unlike the other days, today they both sat facing each other at a proximal distance, holding both hands as if creating a circle of energy to send across the universe that could not be denied and would be replied to.

Gurshamal and Ganga let the universe know, yet again, of their desire to have a child. They expressed their desire with intensity, urgency, and a spirit filled with charged positivity post the puja. Ten years of life together had given them everything except a little being that would call them ma and baba. Ten years had gone by in prayers and tears, in hope and sorrow.

That day, the heavens were finally moved by their faith, steadfast for a decade. That day, the heavens finally decided to relent and birth a miracle.

A few weeks later, the two discovered that Ganga was pregnant. It was a monumental moment that unleashed as many tears as it did smiles. It was a day of happiness so overwhelming that it threatened to tear apart their hearts. In a moment, their lives had completely changed.

The barren land showed signs of life too, all of a sudden. Tiny saplings covered the once-parched land. It seemed as if the miracle that had blessed Ganga's womb had spilt over.

The news of her pregnancy spread through the village. Women, who had once avoided her, now thronged to her house to give advice. Lila, too, visited her one day with her little one.

'You are glowing. It's like looking into the sun!'

Ganga smiled. 'He is growing up so fast, and look at those plump cheeks!' She pulled the infant's cheeks and the baby cooed indulgently.

'Here', said Lila, placing her son in Ganga's lap, 'they say if you play more with a boy, a boy you will deliver'.

While the advice meant little to Ganga, she was more than happy to play with the cherub in her arms.

'And avoid the company of childless women, their bad energy might affect you.'

'Aren't you a sweetheart? Yes, you are! Yes, you are…' Ganga was too occupied with Lila's son to pay any attention to—what she believed was—ill advice.

While Ganga ignored most of the advice she got from the other women, she was grateful for their concern and care. Her neighbours would often drop by with jars of homemade pickles and other delicacies to satiate her cravings and bombard her along the way, with extensive lists of dos and don'ts.

One morning, Rukmani, an eighty-year-old woman with five children and nineteen grandchildren, came by just after Gurshamal had left for the day's work.

'Come, Ganga. Come with me', she said, storming into the house.

'Where, Daadi?'

'Don't ask too many questions, just come.'

Rukmani grabbed Ganga by the hand as though she was a child, and took her to the village temple. The lone banyan tree in the temple courtyard, over a hundred years old, was believed to grant the wishes of those who tied a piece of red thread on it.

Rukmani pulled Ganga closer and whispered in her ear, 'Pray for a healthy boy and a smooth delivery. And don't tell anyone what you wished for.'

Gurshamal left no stone unturned in pampering his beloved wife. He would buy mangoes for her by the dozens and all things sour. He refused to let her do too much work around the house and surprised her often with presents.

Ganga spent her days feeling her swollen belly and heading to the local market to buy the softest wool she could find, in the brightest of colours, to knit pullovers and socks for the little one. The couple could not wait to become parents.

One evening, Gurshamal returned home, looking upset.

'What is wrong? Had a bad day at work?'

'Brats! Monsters! They have no souls! God shall never forgive them! I wonder if they can be called humans... even animals are better than them', Gurshamal spoke, his nostrils flared.

'What happened?'

'There was a barbaric attack by a gang of dacoits yesterday in the neighbouring village. They not only robbed half a dozen houses but also slaughtered six people, two of them women and even a child! One of the two women who died was pregnant. She was trying to escape but was kicked and eventually killed by the horses. What a—'

Gurshamal abruptly stopped as he saw the look of absolute terror on Ganga's face.

'I am sorry, Ganga. I should not have—'

'I would have found out from someone else if not you…what is this village turning into? How will we raise a child in an environment like this?'

Gurshamal shook his head. 'I am fed up with these Mughal invaders and their acts of cruelty to usurp wealth…they have been forcibly converting locals to Islam too. They want to take over the entire region.'

'By slaughtering people and hijacking our faith?'

'The Panchayat has called for a meeting in the evening tomorrow. There is a lot that needs to be discussed.'

The next morning, as Gurshamal left for work, he called Ganga, 'Be ready at four today for the Panchayat meeting'.

Ganga looked at him, puzzled.

'You are coming to the meeting', said Gurshamal calmly.

'Have you forgotten? Women are not allowed to attend Panchayat meetings.'

'And that should change now. Safety is a matter of concern for both the men and women of this village.'

'Which is all true, but they will simply not allow me there!'

'Sit a little further away from us…I will handle it, don't worry. I want you to be there, to hear the discussion, to take part in it, to be assured that you will be safe.'

It was around 3:30 pm when Gurshamal returned from work.

'Ganga, are you ready?' He said as he walked in.

Ganga sat on the charpoy, plaiting her hair. 'Almost done!'

She walked into the courtyard, anxiety written large on her face.

Gurshamal held her hand. Calming her immediately with his quiet assurance, he led her out of the house.

'What will you tell them?'

'About what?'

'About me.'

'Ganga, stop overthinking. It will be okay.'

'I don't want your reputation and goodwill to be questioned on my account.'

'It won't be. Just stop worrying. Stress is not good for the little one, you remember that, don't you?'

The big banyan tree was now visible, and so were the men sitting under it. Ganga felt their eyes bore into her. She could see some of them whisper into each other's ears. She tightened her grip on Gurshamal's hand even as her feet hesitated.

'Let's go, Ganga.'

Gurshamal sat her down barely a few feet away from the circle of men sitting under the tree. He then proceeded to join them. The Sabha began with the head's address.

'…I am happy that you have brought along your wife', he said to Gurshamal. 'The women of this village have a right to know what measures are being taken to ensure that such brutal attacks don't occur again in the future—'

'But the men of this village are competent enough to ensure it does not happen again. Surely, the women of this village need not come here and check whether we are doing our job right!' one of the sarpanch members, Govind, said.

'Whoever has a problem can leave.'

Govind stood up.

'Govindji', said Gurshamal, 'your presence here is paramount, now more than ever, when brutes threaten the peace and harmony of our neighbourhood. Please do not leave. My wife's presence here in no way questions our methods or working. In these dangerous times, maybe it is best to include as many voices and opinions as we can.'

Govind considered for a moment in silence.

'We are all here for one thing and one thing alone— the welfare of the people of this village. No individual or gender is bigger than that goal.'

Govind sat down. The discussion ensued and continued for over an hour. The head concluded the Sabha with yet another address.

'As suggested by the majority, from now onwards, all male members of this village between the age of fifteen and forty will learn the skill of warfare from fellow villagers of the Kshatriya community. If they bring the fight to our homes, they leave us no choice but to fight back.'

Along with the Panchayat's decision, the news of a woman attending the Panchayat Sabha spread through the village like wildfire. On their way back, an old man who sat outside his house on a charpoy called out to Gurshamal, 'Let the ladies take care of the household, why bother them and bring them out of the backyard? Izzat should be kept behind the veil, in the safety of the backyard, just like we keep our cattle.'

Humiliated by the man's comment, Ganga pulled her *odhani* further so that it covered her face entirely. Gurshamal simply smiled and kept walking. Squeezing his wife's hand, he said, 'Let them talk. Don't pay heed to their words. You should be proud. You made history today. I am sure a lot of the women of our village will be motivated to follow in your footsteps'.

Over the next few weeks, the Panchayat's orders began to take shape as *akharas*—practising grounds for wrestling—were built in the village for men to learn and practice warfare skills. Men from all castes would practice together with swords, spears, and lathis. This brought the community closer as men from all castes were suddenly united by a single goal, compelled to spend time together and communicate.

CHAPTER 2

Birth

Summers went, and monsoons began. The earth and Ganga's belly were both flourishing.

One day, while washing dishes, Ganga abruptly halted as she felt a strange movement. Breathing heavily, her gut filling up with anxiety, she slowly got up, hand on her belly. Tears rolling down her eyes, she rushed to Lila's home.

'Lila! Lila!' She frantically knocked on the door.

'What happened, Ganga? What's wrong?'

'I felt something…something bad. Is my baby okay?'

'Calm down. Come inside, drink a glass of water, then tell me—'

'Lila!' Ganga grabbed her by the arm. 'I was washing the dishes when I felt a strange movement in my stomach…as if a ball had wobbled. I am really scared. Is something wrong with my baby? Is it no longer attached to my belly?'

Lila burst out laughing. 'Oh Ganga, relax! It's a good sign! The little one has grown enough to move around and explore his tiny house. Your baby is perfectly healthy.'

Every day brought with it new lessons and experiences for the couple. Ganga could now distinctly feel the movements of her baby. Gurshamal and Ganga would sing to it songs of devotion and tell stories of how the world and the universe came to be, stories of men and women who had shaped the world with their courage.

'What do you think? Are we going to have a boy or a girl?' Ganga asked one day.

Gurshamal shrugged his shoulders. 'It does not matter to me. I would be equally happy to have a boy or a girl.'

'Really?'

'Yes, of course!'

On 27 November, on the ninth phase of the moon, just when both had arisen from sadhana, Ganga felt the contractions begin. Breathing heavily, she said, 'I think it's time. We must call Daayi maa'.

Anxious and overwhelmed, Gurshamal rushed out of the house barefoot and ran back with the elderly woman who had delivered dozens of children in the village. Along with her came Veena and Geeta, two more women from the neighbourhood. While Daayi maa consoled Ganga, the two women followed her instructions to bring hot water and other necessities.

Meanwhile, Gurshamal paced back and forth in the courtyard, reciting Lord Vishnu's name. A few men from the neighbourhood had also gathered there to battle fate and the freezing night in solidarity. Above them, the skies were gathering an ominous blanket of clouds.

Every now and then, Gurshamal would hear a sharp cry of pain from within the house that would make him freeze. The anxiety bubbling within him threatened to tear him apart. Flashes of lightning started to disrupt the darkness of the night.

Ganga was now screaming in pain. She had been in labour for over two hours. Outside, it started drizzling. Some of the men, citing various reasons, walked back to their homes. Some had to eat dinner and some had to go to sleep to start early the next day. Gurshamal now sat by himself, wishing the rains lashed heavier and drowned out Ganga's cries entirely.

Four hours passed. The rains stopped. A lull fell upon the neighbourhood. All sounds from within the house fell silent. Gurshamal had seen many women in the village die during childbirth. He had been to the burial of nearly half a dozen infants, born dead. Fearing the worst, he walked into the house.

The moment he took his first step inside, a loud cry emerged from within the house. His legs drained of all strength, and he slumped to the ground. Tears of joy ran down Gurshamal's cheeks as he heard his baby for the first time. One of the ladies stepped out of the room and said, 'It's a girl'. Her face and tone carried not the slightest hint of happiness.

Seth Gurshamal joined his hands and bowed down

to Lord Vishnu's image in his living room. 'Thank you, Lord', he said, his heart full of gratitude. He stormed into the room and scooped up the infant in his arms. He looked at her lovingly and then at Ganga. 'Thank you, thank you for this gift! This is the happiest day of my life.'

Ganga looked on, overwhelmed at that moment with love for her child and husband. Could she be any luckier?

'I feel as if I am holding the sun itself', Gurshamal told Ganga. 'I cannot believe she is here, after years of praying and hoping…she is finally here!'

The three other women in the room looked on with surprise and shock. They had never seen anyone happy after hearing the news of their wife delivering a girl child.

'Lord Vishnu could not have been more gracious', he said.

Ganga nodded, tears flowing down her cheeks. 'What should we name her?' she asked.

'Since she is a blessing from Lord Narayan himself, we should name her Narayani.'

Ganga smiled. 'Narayani! Narayani is perfect.'

Gurshamal walked over to his wife and gently handed her Narayani. He then stroked her hair gently. 'Our family is complete now.'

That night, the couple did not sleep as they spent all their time looking at their little angel. The moment morning light broke into the house, Gurshamal got ready and headed out. He went straight to the sweet shop and bought four dozen boxes of sweets.

'If all the people in this village were like you and welcomed the birth of their daughters just as much as they did their sons, I would sell a lot more sweets throughout the year', chuckled the shopkeeper as he handed Seth Gurshamal his packet.

Gurshamal went around the village distributing sweets in every household, invoking all kinds of conversations in the process.

'Having a child this late in life...'

'He is good to be a grandfather!'

'...and distributing sweets even though his wife gave birth to a daughter...'

'If it was me, I would not step out of the house for a month!'

'Gurshamal is a fool.'

While most men mocked him, the women, though not vocal, were happy to see him celebrate. Although Gurshamal was aware of the things being said about him, he did not care at all. This was a moment of happiness that he and Ganga had awaited for over a decade. He refused to let the archaic thoughts of his neighbours take away from their moment. Gurshamal was so overjoyed that he even distributed sweets in the neighbouring villages.

Defying social norms, he decided to arrange a grand feast to celebrate the birth of his daughter. Brahmins from far and wide were invited, as were commoners. Hundreds came to bless the girl. Just as everyone sat down for the feast, a renowned seer walked in. 'Alak Niranjan! Let me see the girl whose birth has been announced and received with such zeal.'

The couple bowed before the sage and escorted him to the cradle decorated heavily with flowers. After a moment's silence, he spoke, 'She is destiny's chosen one. Her eyes bear the spark of conviction and innocence… she is a special soul, this one, and she is destined to do great things. The world will look up to her one day with reverence. Gurshamal, you are indeed a blessed man. Your sadhana, good faith, and call to the universe have been answered with this divine girl. Raise her well'.

Narayani became the pivot of Ganga's and Gurshamal's lives. They gave her all their time, energy, and attention. As new parents, they were also quite protective of their little girl. While doing everyday chores such as cleaning utensils, washing clothes, or attending to their cow Amba, Ganga would shift the cradle to ensure that Narayani was always under her watchful eyes.

Teenage girls often visited their home to play with Narayani. Narayani, too, loved the attention. These visitors, however, made Ganga frantic with worry. 'Don't lift her, she may fall!' She would keep reminding them to clean their hands before they touched Narayani. Even Gurshamal was not spared. Days flew by in a blur of happiness and memories.

Ganga and Gurshamal would share the joy of each one of Narayani's milestones with the neighbours. When her first tooth erupted, they distributed sweets. When she first cooed the words 'Baba' and 'Ma', they held a puja. When she stood on her feet for the first time, the entire village was invited to a feast. Narayani made every moment a reason to be celebrated. Her parents would watch her lovingly as she slept between them, hearts brimming with joy and minds full of prayers.

It wasn't long before Narayani started walking by holding on to the charpoy's edge. The very next day after Gurshamal saw her walking, on his usual trip to Hisar, a famous chilli trading town 80 km away from Dokwa, he visited the goldsmith and bought presents for the two women in his life. After he reached home that evening, he first adorned Narayani's feet with the gold anklets he had bought, and then Ganga's.

The anklets appeared to please Narayani as she giggled with every step from then on. Ganga's heart would leap with joy every time she heard the sound of the trinkets on Narayani's ankles, followed by the sound of her laugh. It happened often, too, for Narayani was an extremely active and happy child. She was constantly on the move, discovering the world around her one step at a time. This cheered Ganga up as much as it frightened her. She could not step away from her for too long, for if she did, Narayani would end up falling and bruising herself.

Narayani was rapidly picking up her parents' habits. Every day during sadhana, she sat beside them in silence with her eyes closed. At first, this amused Ganga and Gurshamal, but as they observed her, they realised that it was quite an astonishing feat for an infant. Narayani would sit like an adult without flinching or opening her eyes. In fact, she would continue to sit like that even after her parents had opened their eyes. Yet, for the most part, her antics were but a reflection of her very young age.

She would sit in the washing area and imitate her mother when she cleaned the clothes. In bed, she would put one leg over the other as Gurshamal often did, when he gazed into the distant fields covered in lush greens. When Ganga kneaded dough, Narayani would rush to her immediately and ask for some. She would then roll it between her fingers, stretch it, and smear it all over her palms and clothes. Ganga would smile and sculpt a toy from the dough, a snake sometimes, a human figure other times.

Gurshamal often took her for walks through the fields. Narayani would pull his kurta, point a finger up at the sky and say, 'Baba, Baba'. Gurshamal would immediately lift her, throw her up in the air and catch her. She would laugh heartily. Both father and daughter would play their silly game for as long as Gurshamal's hands did not tire.

This was an unusual sight in the village, for fathers were rarely seen spending time with their children. From time immemorial, it had solely been the mother's job, a thought process that Gurshamal did not subscribe to. He loved spending time with his little one and indulged her whenever he could.

CHAPTER 3

Amba's Moos

Gurshamal and Ganga, while raising Narayani, were now also preparing to welcome a new member to the family. Amba, their heavily pregnant cow, was about to deliver soon. Ganga gave her fresh fodder, made her shed comfortable, and attended to all her needs. Gurshamal called for a labourer to prepare a thatch in the backyard to protect the calf from extreme weather.

One day, Ganga was busy in the backyard preparing a *chulha* with wood and charcoal. Narayani was sitting amidst her wooden toys, lost in her world of make-believe. Ganga called out to her, 'What's my rani *beti* doing?'

Narayani giggled loudly and said, 'Maa!' Assured that her daughter was safe and not being mischievous, Ganga continued her work. After some time, she called out to her yet again, 'Does *bitiya* want Maa to come and play with her?'

Narayani did not respond.

'Can Ma also come and play?' Ganga repeated her words.

There was still no response. Abandoning her work in the storeroom, Ganga rushed out to check on her daughter. To her surprise, Narayani was nowhere to be seen. Her toys, however, were still there, scattered and forlorn. Ganga turned her gaze immediately to the main iron gate. It was closed but unlatched. She scanned the whole courtyard—behind the charpoy, in the wash area, behind the fodder heap—but Narayani was nowhere.

Blinded now by tears, she yelled in despair, 'Narayani! Laado?'

Shouting her name, she rushed inside the kitchen and then the adjacent room where her cradle lay. Overcome by panic, Ganga rushed back to the main gate. Someone had kidnapped her daughter. What would she do now? What would she tell Gurshamal? Just as she was about to step out of the main gate, something caught her attention—among the clothes she had put out to dry in the sun, her red *odhani* was missing.

A thought zipped through her mind and she ran back into the room. She saw it there, sticking out of the corner behind the huge rack. She took a step forward and, to her relief, saw Narayani wrapped in the *odhani*, fast asleep in the little space between the wall and the shelf filled with barrels of grains. Heaving a sigh of relief, she picked her up and held her close to her bosom as tears trickled down. She put her in the cradle and covered her with the red *odhani*—her daughter's favourite. She would often play with it and wrap it around herself. Ganga looked at her daughter lovingly, taking just a moment longer to admire her beautiful little face.

A loud 'moo' from Amba interrupted her thoughts and she rushed out. Amba was going to deliver. The contractions had begun.

Later that evening, when Gurshamal came back from work, he was greeted by the sight of a beautiful female calf. By then, Narayani had woken up. Gurshamal decided to introduce her to the newest family member.

Putting Narayani down in front of the calf, he let his daughter be guided by her own curiosity. Narayani was watching the calf wide-eyed. She started walking towards her with her arm stretched.

'Keep her away, Amba might hurt her!' Ganga yelled, shocked to see that Gurshamal was letting their daughter around a cow that had just given birth.

Gurshamal smiled and said, 'You worry too much. Amba can never hurt our daughter or us. She is a very intelligent being—intelligent enough to identify who is a threat and who is not. Don't worry about Narayani. She will be as safe with her as she would be with us.'

Ganga nodded and smiled. She then watched Narayani pat Amba and the new calf that was struggling to balance itself on its wobbly legs. Narayani was absolutely ecstatic. 'Juggli! Juggli!' She cried, pointing at the calf. The couple decided to name the calf Juggli.

From that day, Narayani found a new friend and

sibling in Juggli. Just as her mother fed Amba, Narayani would attempt to feed Juggli by picking the greenest, most tender fodder, and putting it in a container for her to eat.

'Narayani, she feeds on her mother's milk, not fodder; she is yet to grow teeth', her mother would tell her, bursting out with laughter.

Narayani spent all her time watching and talking to Juggli. She even told her mother to buy Juggli a pair of anklets just like hers. At times, when the calf became restless and started mooing loudly, Narayani would quietly untie her and let her go to Amba, who was tied some distance away from Juggli's thatch.

Ganga was preparing dinner one night. Narayani sat next to Juggli, talking to her, but the calf appeared distracted. Juggli was trying to pull herself towards Amba. Narayani considered for a moment and then spoke in Juggli's ear, 'Juggli, do you want to be with your mother? Is that why you don't want to play with me? My mother has to tie you far from your mother because otherwise, you will keep feeding on your mother's milk even if you are not hungry and waste it. I love to be around my ma too...I am going to let Amba loose but don't make noise, or else Ma will know'.

Narayani let Amba loose. The cow rushed to Juggli and started licking her to calm her. Narayani then went in to join Ganga. Ganga, who was now sitting in deep sadhana, could hear Juggli's sad moos. At the same time, she could smell the milk burning on the *chulha*. She got up abruptly and ran into the kitchen. To her surprise, there was no milk there. Then she heard Narayani's cries from the veranda where she had left her playing with her *odhani*. She could still hear Juggli's sad moos. She looked towards the thatch and saw Amba licking Juggli and pacifying her.

Although perplexed about how they were together, even though she had tied them separately, she decided to address her daughter's howls first. After calming Narayani down, she went to check on Amba but was surprised to see a happy Juggli seated alone and Amba in her designated place, albeit with her rope untied. She was trying to make sense of these instances when Narayani called out to her mother, 'Ma! Ma!'

She went back to her daughter and let her climb into her lap. Narayani began to play with the *odhani* yet again so her mother resumed sadhana. Ganga's thoughts, however, were preoccupied with what had just happened. Several minutes after introspecting, she realised an important thing. She realised that animals, too, just like human beings, craved their mother's love. Just like humans, they craved physical proximity. She was struck by a profound sense of guilt as she had been intentionally keeping Amba away from her daughter just so that her milk could be collected for their personal consumption and barter.

She walked into the kitchen and looked at the milk vessel. Her first thought was to throw it away. Tears flowing down her cheeks, she picked up Narayani and went to the thatch. Taking a deep breath and wiping her tears, she sat down on the ground in front of Amba and spoke, 'I am sorry, Amba! Although I am a mother too, I failed to understand the emotions of the mother in you'.

She looked towards Narayani and spoke, 'It's my little Narayani who understood you and Juggli...she made me realise my fault. I failed you both, and now it's time to make amends'. She then stood up, brought Juggli to Amba, and tied her next to her mother.

'A moment away from my Narayani makes me feel as if my breath has been snatched from my body...I forced that same pain upon you for several weeks for my selfish needs. Please forgive me.'

She then ran her hands on Juggli's back as tears ran down her face. A sense of peace took over her. Narayani, who had been watching her mother, came and hugged her. Juggli nuzzled against her mother's face and mooed loudly.

The next morning, when Gurshamal returned from his trip, Ganga told him at length what had happened. 'I will no longer keep Amba and Juggli separate...' she concluded.

Gurshamal stroked Narayani's hair. 'If not for her, we would have never understood...her empathy is unusual for her age.'

'You remember the seer's words, don't you?'

'I do...to the last word.'

CHAPTER 4

Aanandi's Story

'*Akhand saubhagyawati bhava*', blessed the Pujari as he put vermilion on Narayani's forehead. It was the ninth phase of the moon in the Kartik month. Narayani had turned five. Like every year since her birth, she was at the temple with Ganga and Seth Gurshamal to seek Lord Narayan's blessings and to distribute alms among the poor.

Narayani put her palms together and extended them towards the Pujari. 'My favourite *prasad*, Pandit ji?'

'Which one?' He feigned innocence.

'Have you really forgotten, Pandit ji? The bright yellow, sweet *boondi* soaked in ghee and sugar syrup.' Narayani licked her lips. The Pujari smiled.

'Of course, I remember.'

He filled her tiny palms with a generous helping of the sweet, then placed his hands on her head and said, 'Your forehead bears the *tej* of the sun, and your eyes the calmness of moon. You are very special, my child'.

'Hmm', said Narayani, cheeks swollen with the dumping of the entire treat in her mouth at once. Yet again, she extended her palms towards the Pujari. The old man smiled and obliged. Ganga and Gurshamal watched their daughter's antics with smiles on their faces, bubbling with affection and pride. Once Narayani finished eating the *boondi* to her heart's content, the family walked out of the temple. Outside, to the poor seated beside the temple wall, Seth Gurshamal started distributing white *patasha* and coins.

'Ma, why do we give them all this? We don't even know them', Narayani asked her mother.

Ganga stooped down so that her eyes met her daughter's. 'Narayani, today is a very special day for us. By the grace of Lord Narayan five years ago, your father and I were blessed with your birth. It was the happiest moment of our lives. We give away to the poor on your birthday every year to express our gratitude towards the lord for giving us what we wanted the most. Besides, it is our dharma to receive from and return to the universe.'

On the way back home, Narayani gorged on some more *boondi* while perched atop her father's shoulder.

'Baba', she spoke with her mouth full, 'is it possible to eat so much *boondi* that my stomach bursts open?'

'No, I don't think so.'

'But it is possible to eat so much *boondi* that it gives you a bad stomachache', said Ganga. A little girl of Narayani's age watched the family walk past.

'Ma, I too want to sit on baba's shoulder just like her', she said to her mother standing beside her. 'But I am too scared of him to ask…'

'Your baba will not do that; you know that very well…'

'But why?'

'Because fathers do not play with their children. Their only job is to earn. It is the mother's job to do everything else.'

'But her baba is playing with her…'

'What do you want me to do about that?' She snapped.

Narayani and her parents had long crossed them, their backs growing smaller and smaller by the minute. The little girl sniffed. The mother immediately repented her harsh tone.

'Laado, your baba is not strong like her baba, but your mother is. Come, I will make you sit on my shoulder.'

Narayani and her parents were now out of the little girl's sight.

'Narayani! Aye Narayani! I know it's your birthday, and I can smell the *boondi* from here.'

'Baba, quick! Quick! Let's make haste, or Lila *tai* will satisfy her grumbling stomach with my precious treats.'

'Wait, I am coming to take it all. I will give it all to Kaalu!'

'No, no, don't give it to Kaalu. He will get a bad stomach if he eats this *boondi*. It has all gone bad.'

Narayani's parents burst out laughing. The family

resumed their walk after Lila blessed the little girl. They halted several times on the way to oblige everyone who wanted to give their blessings to Narayani. Nearly an hour after they started from the temple, the family reached home. Narayani hurriedly slid down Gurshamal's shoulder. Holding tight in one hand the packet of prasad that the Pujari had given, she ran towards Amba's thatch. Placing it on the clay floor, Narayani scooped all she could with her tiny palms and held it before Juggli.

'Eat! I know you like it as much as I do.'

The calf nodded and started licking the *boondi* off Narayani's hands, tickling her.

'Laado! Laado!'

Narayani wiped her hands on her *ghaghra*.

'Ma is calling. I will come back and tell you all about my day.'

Ganga held Narayani's hands down on either side. 'Do not move!' She said in a stern voice. Clutching a handful of dried red chillies in her right fist, she began circling them around Narayani's head anti-clockwise, murmuring something inaudible.

'Why are you doing this, ma? I have to play with Juggli. Can I please go?'

Ganga looked at her sternly with a finger on the lips, shook her head, and continued to draw circles over her daughter's head with the chillies. Once done, she put them in the *chulha*, that in turn, stirred up a massive cloud of smoke. Ganga and Narayani both started coughing.

'Close your eyes, Laado! They will burn if you keep

them open.'

Ganga pulled Narayani close to her chest and buried her face in it. After several minutes, once the smoke dispersed and the air turned breathable again, they pulled apart.

'Ma, why did you do all that? For us to cough?'

'You ask too many questions! I did it to remove the negative energy that people might have cast on you. Did you see all that smoke? That means there was loads and loads of it.'

'Loads and loads of chillies?'

'Uff, *nazar*! Now, go and wash yourself.'

'But ma, how come you don't do it for baba?'

'Because he is not a child. He is a grown-up. He won't be affected by anyone's bad energy.'

'But I turned five today, I will not be affected either!'

'Enough questions. Go now! Go wash yourself! One more question and you won't get the rest of the *boondi*.'

Later that evening, after washing herself clean as her mother had instructed, Narayani headed straight to the kitchen. Ganga sat bent over next to the *chulha*, rolling chapattis. Narayani cleared her throat to get her mother's attention.

Ganga looked up. 'Laado, are you hungry? I will serve dinner in ten minutes—'

'Ma, I am here to talk about something important.' Ganga looked at her, bemused. 'I am a grown-up now, ma, look at my hands', she put her hands out as evidence, 'See my palms, they are so much bigger and stronger than before; they can hold and do so much more. Let me cook rotis for baba and you'.

Ganga smiled and pulled Narayani into her lap. Holding her palms, she said, 'Oh my! Laado's hands have certainly grown bigger. They can handle more responsibilities...'

'Yes ma, watch!' Narayani took the rolling pin and dough and started rolling out a chapatti just like she had seen her mother do several times. Gurshamal, who was stooped into his account book, looked up with a smile, overhearing the mother-daughter converse. He looked on with a smile on his face. No matter how hard she tried, Narayani couldn't roll the chapatti into a perfect circle. Soon, tears started rolling down her cheeks.

'It's ok, Laado, you can start all over again', said her mother taking the half-broken chapatti and mashing it together into a ball.

Narayani tried again, this attempt as wasted as the last. 'I...I can't do it, ma! I can't even roll a chapatti...I am useless!'

'Laado, why would you say such a thing!' Her mother pulled her daughter into a hug. 'Silly girl, don't ever think or speak like that! You will learn everything with time... rolling a chapatti, keeping the house in order, all of it.'

During sadhana, Gurshamal stayed preoccupied with a thought stirred by his daughter's words. Later that night, after Ganga and Narayani fell asleep, he stayed up watching Narayani's face.

An old memory wafted in front of his eyes, and he

went back to the time when he was only twelve, watching his recently widowed sister Aanandi, only a year older than him, try to run the house with a belly swollen by seven months of pregnancy.

'Ma has sent some rice for you, and these laddoos.'

'Ay, where is my food? The witch ate my husband and son. Now she will eat me too!' A harsh, nasal voice came from the other room.

Aanandi's father-in-law had passed away shortly after her own marriage to Gopal. Her mother-in-law had been bedridden for three years after a stroke paralysed her waist down. She blamed Aanandi for her son's death, although he had drowned in a well on one of the many nights when he got drunk out of his mind with his friends.

'Why don't you just leave all this and come home? Let her die, she does not deserve to live, and she won't for long...' Gurshamal tried to persuade Aanandi whenever he visited her.

'This is my home now', she would say.

Having never attended a *pathshala* and suddenly burdened with the responsibility of not only running the house but also earning a living, Aanandi was clueless. She tried to find odd jobs, but none lasted long. Men in the neighbourhood tried to take advantage of her helplessness. She would never tell Gurshamal about them, but he knew. When she finally gave birth, things only became worse. With an infant at home, she could no longer go out to work in the fields in exchange for grains and vegetables. Gurshamal would visit her often, carrying with him money and food sent by their mother. As months plodded on, he watched his sister get reduced to a shadow, constantly harassed by her mother-in-law and utterly failing to make a living.

One day, Gurshamal visited his sister's house to tell her that their parents had found a girl for him.

'Oh! My little brother is going to be a *dulha* now! Did you hear that', she said, looking at her baby, who had been crying in her arms long before Gurshamal arrived, 'Your mama is going to get married!'

'Can you silence that monster?' Her mother-in-law yelled. 'That thing cannot be my son's child. He was so quiet and calm! I should have known when neighbours came to tell me that my daughter-in-law is a whore!'

'That's it, you are coming with me right now', said Gurshamal, getting up.

'You know very well that I can't. I'd rather die than go back to our parents' house...anyway, I am useless, with no knowledge of managing the old family shop of grains and no skills to run this house—a failed wife, a failed daughter-in-law, and now a failed mother too, what is the point if I live or die? I am totally useless!'

Gurshamal turned towards Lord Narayan's image, seeking a direction in silence. Just then, Narayani mumbled in sleep, '*Haan* baba'. Startled at first, Gurshamal thought it was the lord directing him through his daughter's words. Relieved, he finally fell asleep and woke up early the next morning. 'You seem unusually happy', said Ganga, watching Gurshamal as he finished his morning chores, 'and in an unusual rush. What is going on?'

'It's a special day, and I have some important work. I will tell you once I finish it.' Ganga smiled lovingly and gave him his *jhola*. Gurshamal headed out of the house, his steps conveying his intent. Instead of heading to the shop, he walked straight to the only *pathshala* in the village, located at the other end.

CHAPTER 5

A Visit to the Pathshala

In a neat courtyard sat a thatched two-room structure. Next to it was a hundred-year-old mango tree.

'So, what do we learn from the story?'

The voices from within the *pathshala* grew louder as Gurshamal approached it. 'We learn, Masterji, that a friend in need is a friend indeed.'

Gurshamal stopped outside the open door. Inside, four boys sat on the floor facing the blackboard and their teacher—a man in his late forties with a paunch and a face riddled with wrinkles. Recognising Gurshamal, he smiled and walked out of the classroom.

'Arre, Seth Gurshamal ji! What a special day this is! Has the sun risen from a different direction? Or have you lost your way? This is a *pathshala*, not a marketplace. What are you doing here?'

They started walking together towards the mango tree.

'Yes Masterji! The sun has indeed risen from a different direction today, and I am here to let you know that it is all my doing.' Gurshamal smiled. They sat down on the bench beneath the tree. 'Masterji, why are so many children absent today?'

'Nobody is absent; there are only four boys in the class', Masterji sighed.

'There have to be at least seventy children in this village who are of school-going age.'

'*Bhaiya*, who believes in knowledge? I built this *pathshala* to spread the light of knowledge. On his deathbed, my father had expressed his desire to open a *shala* where knowledge would be provided to those who seek it. I gave up on my Brahmin ritualistic work and converted my home into this *shala* to fulfil his wish. I realised over time that my efforts alone would not suffice. As a society, there needs to be a change in our mindset towards education. Only the Brahmin and Vaishnava kids come to study. The rest either assist their fathers or while away their time roaming around. On some days, there is only one student in the class. Today is a rare day. Consider yourself lucky to have witnessed it.' He laughed bitterly.

'I commend you for your efforts', said Gurshamal, 'they won't be wasted'.

Masterji shrugged his shoulders. 'Tell me, how can I help you?'

Gurshamal took a deep breath. 'I want you to give lessons to my daughter Narayani. She is at the right age to begin her education.'

Masterji looked on, bewildered. 'You do know that in our society, girls don't go to study.'

'I do. But I also know that our society needs to change.'

'Gurshamal, the villagers will create a huge ruckus. Your family might be threatened too. This is against the social constructs put in place by our forefathers...'

'I am willing to fight if I need to.' Masterji fell quiet. 'Didn't you say that it was your father's wish to impart knowledge to those who sought it? Didn't you say that our mindset towards education ought to change?'

Masterji spoke after a brief pause, 'I want to meet her once...before I take her as my student.'

Gurshamal could not contain his happiness. 'I will bring her tomorrow to meet you. Narayani is a bright child. She will not disappoint you. Thank you so much! Thank you so, so much!'

Back in his shop, distraction intruded on Gurshamal's work. He could not wait to share the big news with his wife and daughter. He closed the shop before evening fell that day, and hurried back home. On the way, he stopped at the marketplace and bought a slate, chalks, and a small bag. He concluded his shopping with a big parcel of jalebis.

'Ganga! Laado! Come quickly! I have a surprise for both of you.'

Narayani came running, followed by Ganga. 'You are home early today. Is everything alright?'

'Everything is fantastic.'

She looked at his exuberant face and then at his hands holding school supplies. 'What is all this for?'

Gurshamal ignored his wife and looked straight at Narayani. 'These are all for you.'

'But I don't know what to do with them—except for the jalebi', she said, patting her stomach.

'You will take them to the *pathshala*.'

'*Pathshala?*' Narayani asked.

'What are you talking about?' Ganga was puzzled.

'From tomorrow, our Laado will go to the *pathshala* and learn to read and write.'

'Baba, what is a *pathshala?*'

'She is a girl. What will she do in a *pathshala?*'

'A *pathshala* is a place that teaches you about the world and prepares you to face it', Gurshamal first addressed his daughter. He then looked at his wife. 'She will study there just like boys do.'

'What are you saying? Girls don't go to *pathshalas*. Girls don't study. Their place is in the kitchen, at home, cleaning and cooking and taking care of—'

'Ganga, I will not change my decision. Our daughter will get educated.'

'Do you realise that the whole society will stand up against us for this?'

'Here, Laado, take this jalebi and your study supplies. Why don't you go and play with Juggli?' Gurshamal said.

After placing the slate and chalk in her bag, she swung it over her shoulders. She then opened the box of sweets, grabbed a few jalebis in both hands and walked out humming a tune. Breathing heavily, Ganga watched her daughter as she left the room. Gurshamal watched his wife in silence. He had never seen her this angry. Narayani squatted in front of Juggli.

'Baba got us a special treat today', she said, extending her hands towards the calf. 'And he also got me some more things. They are in this bag. I will show you once you finish eating. He says that from tomorrow, I will go to a *pathshala* to learn. But I don't understand—to learn what? I don't even know what a *pathshala* is, do you?'

'Ganga, why are you so upset?' Gurshamal broke the silence. 'Our Laado will learn to read and write…she will be able to read scriptures, do calculations. She is such a bright child. Don't you think we will commit a grave injustice by confining her to the four walls of our home and limiting her many talents? And yes, I do not want to repeat the mistake my father made. If only my sister Aanandi was learned, she would have had a better life for herself and her child.'

'I don't know what to say…I am scared that something untoward might happen to her. No one in the village is going to be happy about this.'

'Trust me, only good things will happen if our Laado goes to study. Masterji is a learned, good man; he will teach her well. As for the villagers, you remember when you attended the Panchayat for the first time?'

'But we are talking about our child here!'

Gurshamal sighed. 'Do you think I will ever let any

harm come to her?' She shook her head in silence. 'You have told me so many times, "I wish I could read, write, and calculate like you do, and help you with your work". Imagine Narayani fulfilling your dream. She will assist not only her mother but her father as well.'

'A girl going to a *pathshala* to learn calculations to assist her father...I know I could not bear you a son, but Laado can't be a son, no matter what she does. Everyone wants a son to take forward the family's name and perform the last rites of their parents. Narayani, being a girl, will not be able to do all those things. We have to accept it...' Tears rolled down her cheeks as she spoke.

'Do not ever again shame the birth of my daughter! She is my pride, irrespective of her gender. And I want to raise her so, without the gender constructs defined by society. Lord Narayan gave her to us. And Lord Narayan brought about a change in hackneyed traditions and blind beliefs of our society. It is only right to raise his gift to us with the same ideals that he holds supreme. If you support me in my cause, well and good; if not, I will fight you along with the rest of the society.'

She fell at his feet. 'You are right. Forgive me, please. I was so rude and...'

Gurshamal raised her by her arms. 'As a mother, you are bound to react the way you did. You do not have to apologise.'

'Narayani is a boon from the Lord himself; you are absolutely right', she spoke, 'we ought to raise her so.'

Later that night, after dinner, lying between Ganga

and Gurshamal at night, Narayani bombarded her parents with questions.

'Baba, what will I learn at the *pathshala*? Who is Masterji? Will there be other children? Can ma come with me?'

Stroking her head gently, Gurshamal explained, '*Bitiya*, a teacher is even higher than god.'

'Really?'

'Yes.'

'God gives us life, but a teacher teaches us the way to live life responsibly and righteously. He sets us in the right direction to lead a life that is beneficial to the world and mankind.'

'Laado, always respect your teacher and follow his teachings well', said Ganga, 'and don't forget to teach your mother too.' Laughter ensued, and soon, the three fell asleep.

The next morning, Ganga dressed Narayani and put two neat braids in her hair. Taking Lord Narayan's blessings first and then her mother's, Narayani walked out of the house holding her father's hand. Lila, who was sweeping the front courtyard, saw Narayani and shouted, 'Ae Narayani, where are you headed dressed like a rani? Your new bag is beautiful. Bring some gifts for me from the market, won't you?'

'Lila *tai*, I am going to a *pathshala*, not to shop at the market. Baba says we get knowledge there. Should I bring that for you?'

Hearing her words, Lila dropped her broom and

looked on in shock. Other people who had heard Narayani started talking.

'Gurshamal has completely lost his mind.'

'I feel bad for him. He thinks his daughter can learn and assist him in trading.'

'His wife could not give him a boy. Poor man!'

Radha, Lila's youngest daughter, who stood beside her, asked, 'Ma, what is a *pathshala*? Why is everyone feeling bad for Gurshamal *tau*? Is he taking Narayani to a dangerous place to convert her into a boy?'

Ignoring her, Lila rushed to Ganga's house. Radha followed her mother. 'Ganga, have you lost your mind? Narayani is going to the *pathshala*? Have you forgotten that she is a girl? You are not even a Brahmin! Her place is beside you in the house, not outside, next to her father. Who will approve of a girl who is educated? Don't you want her to get married someday?'

Ganga looked at her in stoic silence. Knowing that an argument would be futile, she shrugged her shoulders and said, 'Narayani's father knows what is best for her.'

'But ma', said Radha, 'how does a *pathshala* change a girl into a boy? Narayani will now become Narayan?'

'Shut up, you idiot! Don't use your brains. They are meant for the menfolk, not you.' Realising that Ganga appeared unfazed by the allegations, Lila threw her hands up in the air. 'God help that little girl and give some *sadbuddhi* to her crazy parents!'

Holding her father's hand, head held high and face shining like the sun, Narayani finally reached the *shala*.

'That is your Masterji', said Gurshamal and led Narayani towards the mango tree under the shade of which sat Masterji.

'Namaste Masterji', said Gurshamal, 'this is my daughter, Narayani.'

She touched Masterji's feet and spoke, 'Namaste Masterji! I have come to learn from you and gain knowledge. Baba told me that you are above the lord...I promise to obey and follow all your teachings well.'

Masterji smiled and put his hand on her head. 'Bless you, my child. Your father was right about you. It would be my honour to teach you to read and write.'

'Narayani, study well. I will pick you up in a few hours', Gurshamal said and walked away.

'That is your classroom. Go right in and wait there along with the rest of the class. I will be there in a few minutes', said Masterji, pointing to the other room. As Narayani approached the room, she saw a massive black patch on one of the walls with something in white written on it. In front of it, on the floor, sat three boys. The moment Narayani entered the door, hearing her footsteps, they all turned around.

'What are you doing here?'

'Must be lost or something...'

'Look, she has a bag!'

'Yes, baba got it for—'

'Oh yes, she does have a bag! Are you here to study?'

'Yes, baba sent—'

The boys gasped.

'Go home and cook. Shoo!'

The class erupted into laughter.

Narayani looked on, trying to find the right words to defend herself, but all that escaped from her were hot tears of humiliation. She turned around to look for her baba, hoping that he would still be there and they could go back home. Knowing it was a futile wish, she wiped her tears with her *odhani*. 'Your place is inside the house like cows and buffaloes, not like horses and camels out in the market.'

'Shut up, you idiots!' Masterji's thundering voice silenced the room. 'You have all learnt nothing from me, absolutely nothing! There is too much trash filled in your bloated heads. She will sit among you and study like the rest of you; anyone with a problem can leave my classroom. If I hear one more word against her presence in class, it will be you, not her, who will go home.' He turned to his newest student. 'Go take your place, Narayani. I will come back in a few minutes.'

Narayani sat down on the floor. The boys took turns glaring at her and then had hushed discussions. Masterji returned to the classroom and walked to the front. He placed a sculpture on the table in front of the blackboard. He then asked Ved, his oldest student, 'Stand up and tell me whose sculpture it is'.

Ved stood up and bowed down to the statue. 'It is the statue of Goddess Saraswati, the goddess of knowledge.'

'What is she holding?'

'She is the Devi of *gyaan*, holding a scripture and a veena.'

'All of you come here.'

The three boys and Narayani walked to the front.

'Put your arms forward and show me your palms.'

They all followed his instructions.

'Do you see any difference in the hands? Ved? Atharv? Mohan?'

'No', they spoke meekly.

'Then why do you feel that only certain hands are supposed to do certain things? What makes your hands so special that only they can hold books?'

The ensuing silence conveyed the boys' guilt. They looked at each other and spoke in unison, 'We are sorry for our behaviour, Narayani. Please forgive us!'

Narayani smiled. 'It is ok, *bhaiya*.' The class resumed as usual.

Meanwhile, in Gurshamal's home, a stream of visitors kept walking in. The news of Narayani going to the *pathshala* had spread through the village like wildfire. Everyone was annoyed. Brahmins threatened the couple, traders reminded Gurshamal of his boundaries, and others pitied them for not having a son. Gurshamal handled every raised voice in a humble yet firm tone.

'Isn't it time to bring her back from school?' Ganga asked for the fourth time in an hour.

'No, time is moving slowly today…'

Finally giving in, he reached school twenty minutes early to pick Narayani up. Hiding behind the half-open door of the classroom, he watched his daughter as she practised writing. 'Narayani! It is your first day.

You cannot learn everything in a single day. You can do the rest tomorrow.' His youngest student had been relentlessly practising writing. Paying little heed to his words, she continued to write. Gurshamal was amazed by his daughter's dedication.

Holding her slate, she approached her teacher, 'Masterji, I don't think I have done a very good job. I will go home and practice more till I write better'.

Patting her back, he replied, 'I am very proud of your efforts, Narayani! Now go home. I can see your father hiding and watching from outside'. Gurshamal blushed and came out of his hiding spot. Narayani touched her teacher's feet and rushed outside.

'Baba, you know what happened today…' The two held hands and started walking. 'Ved bhaiya, Atharv bhaiya, and Mohan bhaiya teased me a lot…'

On and on, she kept telling her father about the day's happenings as they walked back home. Ganga had been pacing outside the house. She ran to Narayani as she saw them coming and hugged her tight.

'Laado, are you alright? No going to study from tomorrow; I missed you too much. Enough of all this about learning and education.'

Placing her hand on her mother's shoulder, she spoke like her father, 'Ganga! You worry too much. I am fine'. From there, Narayani could hear the constant sound of bells on Juggli's neck. She ran inside to meet her, eager to recount the day's happenings to her.

Radha, who was eavesdropping with her ear placed

against the boundary wall from their adjoining house, could no longer hold back her curiosity. She walked to Narayani's house without informing her mother, Lila. 'Look who is here, Narayani!' Ganga called out to her daughter as Radha walked in.

'Come, Radha. Ma has bought a lot of clay from the market, so let's play with it. I will make a pot, and you?' Narayani asked as they sat down in the courtyard.

'Umm, a doll?'

While Narayani started kneading the dough with her hands, Radha watched Narayani's *jhola*.

'I...can I...will you show me what you took to *pathshala* in that?' She finally spoke.

Delighted by the request, Narayani put the clay aside and showed her friend her school supplies. 'Here', said Narayani offering a piece of chalk to her, 'draw on this slate'.

Radha gasped. She had never seen such a thing. 'No, no! What if it breaks?'

'It won't.' Narayani took the chalk from her and wrote the first Hindi alphabet that she had learnt to write in school that day. 'Why don't you try?'

Radha's face lit up, and this time, she extended her hand to take the chalk from Narayani. Just then, Radha heard Lila's voice. 'Do not let ma know that I was here', she said before running to her house.

'Where were you? What were you doing?' Narayani could hear Lila clearly. 'So much work is left. Go prepare the *chulha* for dinner. Your brother and father will be hungry. And stay away from that house; those people have gone mad.'

The next day, at the Panchayat meeting, Masterji and Gurshamal faced the wrath and questions of the entire village. An elderly Brahmin man spoke first, 'After making your wife and other women in the village attend Panchayat meetings, you now want to open the doors of a school to a non-Brahmin child and that too a girl. Gurshamal, do you think you are about the laws and traditions of our village? What agenda are you carrying in your mind?'

'Neither are we trying to trespass into another caste's territory, nor have we lost respect for our culture and traditions. All that we are doing is opening the doors of knowledge for everyone. If we truly understand our religion and traditions, it is never biased towards any caste. We created these boundaries. Today, if we let our girls learn to read and write just like we do our boys, it will further us as a society', said Gurshamal.

'I am a Brahmin with knowledge of all the Vedas. If even the Vedas do not dictate that *gyaan* is meant for a specific gender or caste, then who are we to decide?' Masterji spoke. 'I request you all to see this as an initiative to bring progress and prosperity to our society, not as a step to break a law or a tradition. It was with your support that I established the school, and I seek from you now that same unflinching support.'

The debate raged on for over an hour, with the majority still standing against Masterji and Gurshamal.

The conclusion, however, came in their favour as Sarpanchji announced, 'Getting educated is not a crime. We have no ground to bar Narayani or any other girl child from going to school. Let light and knowledge prevail'.

Narayani continued going to *pathshala* every day. She would practice and revise all her lessons with her father on the way, oblivious to the glares of many villagers. Children from the village often came up to her and asked her to show them her books, ensuring that they were never caught in the act by their parents or neighbours. 'If we come to your house, Narayani, will you show us how to read and write? We want to go to study too, but our parents won't allow us. Will you be our teacher?'

Gurshamal would feel overwhelmed every time he heard a child say such a thing. It was heartbreaking for him to see a child eager to learn but unable to go to school. Radha would sneak out of her house daily to learn from Narayani. Together, they would practice writing on the floor with charcoal and would mould numbers from clay. Every week, their little school grew in numbers. 'Guru Narayani', as she made all the children call her, was turning out to be as good a teacher as she was a student.

She was like a sponge, her thirst for knowledge insatiable. Going to school became her favourite part of the day. With a keen teacher by her side willing to answer her every question with patience and knowledge, she was unstoppable.

CHAPTER 6

The Good Omen

'*Raghukul neeti sada chali aayi, pran jaaye par wachan na jaaye*', Masterji recited one day in class.

Before he could explain further, Narayani spoke, 'Yes! Promises are to be kept, irrespective of age, *yug*, or birth. Lord Krishna should keep his, and I shall mine'.

Confusion writ large on his face, Masterji looked at her. 'What? What did you say? Which promise?'

As if jolting out of a trance, she looked on, even more confused than he was. 'Masterji...I...what...'

'Pay attention now', Masterji said and continued the story of Ramayana. Narayani often interjected with questions, some of which left her teacher stunned, for they indicated that her understanding surpassed her age. She would enquire about the geographical location of Lord Ram's empire, his journey into various forests during exile and the moral implications of his actions.

Together with the characters of the story of

Ramayana, she experienced a wide array of emotions. She would laugh and clap her hands on hearing about Hanuman's mischiefs, break into tears when Ram, Sita, and Lakshman left for exile, and turn red with rage when Ravana tricked Sita and kidnapped her. She would carry these emotions back home with her every day and recount the story to her usual audience—Ganga, Gurshamal, Juggli, Radha, and other children from the village. One day, while Narayani was narrating the *Lanka Kand* to five children from the village, Lila walked into their home.

'Radha! Aye Radha! Where are you? So much work is left, the *chulha* is not ready, and your father is going to skin you alive…'

Radha did not turn around. Narayani continued her narration. Ganga, who was also sitting there and listening to her daughter, glared at Lila and put a finger to her lips. She gestured for her to take a seat. Stunned by the indifference to her anger, Lila sat down. Although unwilling and annoyed at first, she eventually started listening to Narayani's narration. Just like everyone else in the room, she became so engrossed that she completely lost track of the world around her. Every sound around her except Narayani's voice faded out as she travelled to a different land at a different time.

'Lila! LILA!' She looked up, the spell on her broken. Ganga was shaking her by the shoulders. 'Ae Lila! Where are you?' Before Ganga could explain her actions, Lila heard her husband's voice full of rage. 'He has called you half a dozen times already', said Ganga.

Lila got up swiftly, grabbed her daughter's arm, and ran. Later that afternoon, when her husband returned to the fields, Lila spoke to her daughter. 'So you have been sneaking out to take lessons from Narayani?' She asked, pulling her ear. 'Have you forgotten where you belong? If your father finds out, he will break all your bones. I am giving you one last warning. Stop going to that house.'

Radha started crying. 'What is wrong in learning, ma? I fulfil all my duties, don't I? I love to study, so why won't you let me?'

Moved by her daughter's tears, Lila's heart and tone changed. 'Laado, we are girls. Our only dharma is towards household duties…' Radha listened to her mother, her head bowed, sobbing. 'Society will never accept a girl who goes against the rules set by it…' Radha kept sobbing. Lila stepped forward and enclosed her daughter's face in her hands. Wiping her tears, she said, 'You really love to learn, don't you?'

Radha nodded without uttering a word. Lila sighed. 'Ok then…if it makes you happy, you have my permission to go to Narayani's house and learn. But don't forget your boundaries and make sure no one else comes to know, especially your father.'

Radha looked up, tears of happiness and gratitude flowing down her cheeks. She hugged her mother tight. 'Thank you, ma!'

The next day, yet again at Narayani's house, Radha and other children from the village had gathered to hear the story of Ramayana. Halfway through it, Lila sneaked in and joined the audience. Narayani narrated with great emotion the moment when a stubborn Sita refused to let her husband Ram go into exile alone. Nothing would change her mind about accompanying her husband even though she was not the one sentenced to exile. Elders wailed and begged her, and she responded thus— '*Raghukul neeti sada chali aayi, pran jaaye par wachan na jaaye*', Narayani continued.

'During the *saat pheres* of marriage, I promised to stand beside my husband under any and all circumstances, however trying. Since I belong to the Raghu Clan, I shall keep my promise, even if it means losing my life.'

People started noticing a distinct difference in the thinking of children who were often seen going to Narayani's house. They would talk about religion and high moral values and appeared to possess, in general, an outlook on life that defied their age. Soon the secret unravelled—Narayani was reciting scriptures to them. Word started spreading through the village, and some people started enquiring about sending their children to school.

There were still some naysayers. Some feared that their daughters and wives would forget their duties and move into what was Brahmin territory. The Brahmins, especially, felt threatened. If everyone became learned, no one would seek and revere them. A group of arrogant Brahmin boys, who largely remained aloof from members of the society belonging to other castes, decided to teach Narayani a lesson and remind her of her place. One afternoon after school, while Narayani was returning home with other kids, one of the boys called out to her, 'You think you are a guru now? That taking lessons can make you a Brahmin? Now, you plan to lead society? You little *Janana*!'

'I think I can become whatever I decide to', she replied, unfazed.

The group of four boys walked towards her. 'That is one big mouth that you have', said one of the boys and pulled her *choti*. The other kids with Narayani, sensing the ominous intents of the boys, ran to get help.

'Look at the little cowards running away!' One of the boys laughed.

'Who is going to help you now, Narayani?'

He aggressively pushed her and she fell to the ground. Her *jhola* fell beside her. One of the boys tore open her *jhola* and took out her books. Knowing what was about to happen next, gathering all her strength, Narayani stood up and charged at him. By then, he had already torn her book into two.

'How dare you!' She thundered, head-butting him to the ground. One of the boys then pulled her by the *choti* so that she stood up, while another slapped her several times. They then pushed her yet again, and she fell to the ground a second time. A small stone cut into her knee, and she started bleeding. Unfazed, she picked up a few rocks and started flinging them at the boys.

One of the stones hit one boy in the head, making him bleed. 'Get away from her, you scoundrels!'

The boys turned to their right to see a group of angry villagers approaching them. Narayani continued to hurl stones at the boys till they fled. 'Narayani! Are you alright?' She lay on the ground injured, her bag torn and books scattered.

'What a strong girl. She alone was enough to drive the four of them away!'

'Let's go home now, child.'

Narayani got up, picked up her torn bag and collected her books while tears of anger and humiliation ran down her cheeks. Her mind was racing with angry thoughts— *These are our so-called bearers of knowledge, these boys who attacked me for learning and sharing my gift with others, these cowards!* Seething with rage, she began running towards the village.

'Narayani, wait, let us take you home. You are hurt!' The villagers shouted after her, but she ignored them all and kept running. Huffing and panting, Narayani reached Durga's house—the ironsmith's daughter.

'Durga! Ae Durga! Bring me your father's sword and lathi.'

Durga looked at Narayani in shock, at her tattered clothes and bleeding knee. 'What happened to you, Narayani? Is everything okay?'

'Everything is not okay, which is why I am asking you for your father's sword and lathi to avenge those who have done this to me', she spat.

Durga rushed in and brought her a glass of water.

'Here, Narayani, drink this…'

Narayani threw the glass in rage. 'I asked you for the sword and lathi, not water.'

Ranjit, Durga's elder brother, was listening to their conversation. He brought the sword. 'This is what you want, right? Here, hold it!'

As Narayani took it from him, it fell from her hands.

'You think you are so talented that you can fight with a sword, but you don't even have the strength to lift one! Go home, pick up the rolling pin, and do your chores. This is not one of your flimsy books. One needs years of training to pick and use one of these.'

He stooped down, lifted the sword with pride, and swung it in a swift motion as if cutting the air into pieces. Fuming, Narayani went home. Ganga had just learnt from the villagers what had happened. She paced the courtyard in a state of great anxiety. The moment she saw her daughter approaching, Ganga ran and hugged her daughter tight.

'I told your father not to mess with society's laws and hierarchies...', she cried. 'What if something more serious had happened to you?'

Narayani pushed her mother away.

'You are blaming baba and not the boys who did this to me?'

'No, it's not like that...'

Sobbing, Narayani ran inside the house. Her mother followed. 'Narayani, I am sorry...'

Still crying, Narayani narrated the whole incident to her mother.

'Tell me, ma, what wrong did I do that they felt threatened enough to corner and harm me? Saraswati, the goddess of *gyaan*, is a woman. Yet they say it is not meant for me? They tried to show me my place by outnumbering me in strength and power. What cowards, ma!'

Enraged, Ganga wiped her daughter's tears.

'You are right, Laado, and there is only one way to deal with this. We need to widen your education. You need to learn to handle a weapon, defend yourself, and attack if needed. You will continue to learn, and you will fight those who try to come in your way.'

The next day, Ganga visited Durga's house and requested her father, who headed the *akhara*, to teach defence skills to Narayani.

'Your daughter may be good at studies, but fighting is an entirely different skill. Girls cannot fight even if they try.'

Ganga told him all that had transpired the day before.

'My daughter fought off four older boys; that's all I know. What she may lack in physical strength, she carries in conviction...she is destined for greatness, I know this much by now, and I am here to ask you to help her reach her destiny.'

'Humph. Fine. Bring her to me tomorrow.'

That evening, Gurshamal, who had been away on a trading trip to Hisar, entered the house seething with rage. 'Laado! Ganga!'

The two came running.

'Baba!' Narayani cried on seeing her father and hugged him tight.

'I know what happened. I will see that the perpetrators do not get away with it. Tomorrow we will go to the Panchayat and report the matter. The boys will pay for their crime.'

'You have just returned from a long trip. You must be tired. Let me get some water for you', Ganga said, walking into the kitchen.

'Baba, sit. I have to tell you something important. Ma said that similar incidents can happen again...'

'There are a lot of people in the village who will have a problem with our Laado going to school', Ganga said, handing over the glass of water to her husband. 'I convinced Durga's father to teach Narayani self-defence. That's the best way to deal with this problem. Being self-reliant is the best security we can provide to our daughter.'

The next day, Ganga and Narayani went to Durga's house, and together, they left for the *akhara*. From a distance, Narayani could see a circular, fenced ground. The soil appeared moist and darker than the soil outside the perimeter of the ground. On a charpoy sat Durga's father in an upright posture, shouting instructions in a voice as powerful as the roar of a lion. On a wooden stand lay swords, *lathis*, and *bhaalas*. A few boys were sharpening swords on rocks, often stopping to check the blade with their fingers. Two boys were practising moves with *lathis*, their bare upper bodies drenched in sweat. Ghanshyam thundered, 'With this speed, the opponent will throw you on the ground and bury your face in the soil'.

Seeing Narayani and Ganga, Ghanshyam signalled to the wrestlers to stop. 'This is my daughter, Narayani', said Ganga.

Narayani took a step forward. 'Tell me, *tau*, what do I have to do, I am prepared—'

Ghanshyam pushed her feet with his leg, making her fall to the ground. 'First, learn to stand and hold your ground.'

Although shaken, she stood up dusting her clothes.

'Good! At least you know how to get up with grace after taking a fall. We will begin with unlearning first and then learning will follow.'

His stern demeanour made Ganga nervous. 'Laado, are you ok?'

'Let her be. In order to fight, she will have to understand pain. From tomorrow, you will drop her, and leave. A mother weakens the child. And there is no place for weakness in a fight.'

'*Tau*, my mother is not my weakness, she is my strength', Narayani retorted.

Ignoring her, Ghanshyam instructed both Durga and Narayani, 'Both of you go and run around the ground till I ask you to stop'. Both did as instructed. While Durga, being heftier and sturdier than Narayani, ran with ease, Narayani began panting after a few rounds. She would often slow down to catch her breath. Ghanshyam would yell, 'Did I ask you to stop?'

She stumbled a few times and even fell a couple of times. Every nerve and cell inside her screamed, 'Leave it. Quit. You don't have to do this'.

Yet she kept going. 'I can, I will!' She kept murmuring, recalling the incident when the boys had bullied her with strength.

Ranjit, who stood next to his father, laughed, 'Baba, why waste your time on Vaishnav blood? They do not have the strength for warfare'.

His father glared back at him. 'Strength is not just in the blood but also in conviction. I can already see it in her eyes and moves.'

Ranjit shook his head and walked away. Narayani returned home after an hour, her clothes and hair covered in sand, and immediately collapsed on the bed. Ganga pressed her legs and uttered a silent prayer, 'Lord Narayan, give her the strength to tread the path you have chosen for her. And give me the strength to see my Laado suffer'.

The next morning, while Narayani was getting ready for *pathshala*, Rupa rushed into their house. 'Ganga! Ganga! *Bitiya*, where is your ma? Please inform her that there is a Satyanarayan Katha at my house today. You all must come.'

She turned around to leave but stopped in her tracks. 'Could you…could you ask your mother to prepare some prasad for the puja? We had a failed harvest this year. This puja is to seek blessings and pray to the lord to help us. I shall return the favour.'

'Sure, *tai*! Ma will be happy to help…I will prepare the prasad for the puja myself. Lord Narayan never ignores my prayers. I am his favourite.'

'Bless you, my girl.'

Later that day, seeing Narayani return early from the *pathshala*, Ganga inquired, 'Laado, you are back early today. Are you not feeling well?'

'I will tell you why I am early, wait ma.'

Narayani went inside the room, washed herself, and walked into the kitchen. Climbing onto the stool, she spoke, 'Rupa *tai* came in the morning to invite us for a Satyanarayan Katha'.

'Oh!'

Taking down the massive *kadhai* that sat on the topmost rack, she said, 'Without your permission, I offered to make prasad. I am sorry, ma'.

Taking the *kadhai* from Narayani, Ganga spoke, 'Do you think your delicate hands can prepare prasad for fifty people? Your initiative scares me, Laado.'

'Ma, you worry too much. Besides, I am Lord Narayan's favourite. I could not disappoint him by not making *sooji sheera*…'

Ganga smiled, and together, they prepared prasad while humming songs. A tiring two hours later, the two cleaned up and got ready to go to Rupa's house. Narayani wore her favourite red dress and walked alongside her mother, holding the prasad in a steel container. The moment they entered the house, Panditji remarked in a manner most acidic, 'Here comes the chief guest,

Gurshamal's daughter herself! How privileged are we all to have her grace this occasion with her presence!'

Narayani looked up at her mother and understood her silence well. *Don't say anything.*

Narayani walked straight to the lord's image kept in front. After offering her reverences to the lord, she turned towards Panditji. 'Panditji, here is the prasad.'

'Did you make it?'

'Yes, with my mother's help.'

Panditji began reciting the mantras. Once the Katha was over, Narayani, who was sitting with her hands joined and eyes closed, began to recite the *Vishnu Shahtranam.*

'*Suklambaradharam visnum sasivarnam caturbhujam prasannavadanam dhyayet sarvavighnopasamtaye.*'

Her sweet voice, laced with utmost devotion and clarity of dialect, left everyone spellbound. As the echo of Lord Vishnu's name filled the air, the weather outside began to change its face; the sun mellowed as clouds covered the sky. A gentle breeze started flowing. Plants and trees started rustling in rhythm with Narayani's voice. Everyone closed their eyes and started swaying like the trees outside, mesmerised by her chants. Even Panditji was amazed. As the Stotras ended, everyone bowed down, speaking in chorus,

'*Om Narayan Namah!*'

Just then, it started raining. Everyone received it as a good omen—an answer to their prayers. Rupa's eyes filled with tears in reverence. The lord had heard her prayers. Everyone gathered around Narayani and Ganga, praising the prasad.

'It is so delicious!'

'This is what *amrit* must taste like...satiates the taste buds as well as the soul.'

Panditji blessed Ganga.

'I was wrong about your family and your daughter. She truly is a divine child, above and beyond the petty rules we created. You are blessed; raise her well. She is a boon, not only to your family but to the whole village.'

Narayani and her family started gaining more and more acceptance in the village. Men started seeing women as humans capable of taking charge of matters both inside and outside the house. It became common to see more and more women attend the Panchayat Sabha. Nearly two dozen children went to school now. Parents started encouraging their children to play with Narayani and learn from her. She was looked upon as the ideal child.

In *the pathshala*, Masterji began a new, important lesson. As he laid the new scripture on the table, all the children bowed down in reverence and spoke in chorus, 'Hail Ma Saraswati!'

'Mahabharata, written by the legendary Ved Vyas, is the bulkiest epic in the world. It contains the *gyaan* of the Bhagavad Gita, a source of answers to all questions that arise in a human mind seeking the path to a righteous life full of dharma and karma. Hailing back to the *Dvapara Yuga*, the epic contains the biggest and most heinous war of Kurukshetra. The battle witnessed the bloodshed of almost 1.66 billion warriors, including the fall of legendary warriors like Bhishma, Guru Dronacharya, Karna, the Kuru princes, the young Abhimanyu and many more...'

Hearing the name Abhimanyu sent a chill down Narayani's spine.

'Abhimanyu! Who was he, Masterji? What is his story? How did he die?' She interjected.

Ignoring her misconduct, Masterji replied, 'Of all the names mentioned, why are you so keen on Abhimanyu's story?'

'I...I don't know, Masterji, the name sounds familiar, as if it is related to my story. The name calls out to me...' She fell into a confused silence. Giving into her curiosity and childlike demand, Masterji began to narrate the scene of Abhimanyu's death.

CHAPTER 7

Pre-Life

In the Kali Yuga, around 3102 BCE, the Pandavas and Kauravas were fighting in the Battle of Kurukshetra. The conflict arose between the cousins to settle the claim to the throne of Hastinapur. Every day, the dynastic struggle spilt the blood of hundreds and thousands of warriors. On the tenth day, the battle witnessed the fall of one of its greatest warriors when Arjuna grievously injured Bhishma. With their commander-in-chief now no longer capable of fighting, Kauravas appointed Drona as Bhishma's successor.

Together with their new commander-in-chief, Kauravas decided to implement the chakravyuha—a brilliant and lethal military tactic—to strike the Pandavas with a fatal blow. From the Pandavas, only Arjuna and Krishna had the knowledge required to break and survive the chakravyuha. Realising that the two could render their strategy futile, the Kauravas slyly lured Arjuna away from the chakravyuha along with Krishna, his charioteer.

Faced now with this looming threat that could considerably reduce their army's size, the eldest of the Pandu brothers, Yudhishthira, grew worried. Abhimanyu—Arjuna and Subhadra's sixteen-year-old son—was moved deeply by the plight of his uncle. 'What makes you so worried?' He asked Yudhishthira. 'I, son of the legendary archer Arjuna, shall go to the battlefield and break the deadlock, for I am skilled enough to do so. I shall return triumphant, making the enemies look like fools.'

While overwhelmed by their young nephew's words and enthusiasm, Yudhishthira and Bhima felt unsure. After all, he was just a young boy with little experience of life and lesser so of the battlefield. Abhimanyu, sensing his uncles' hesitance, spoke again, 'Do not be misled by my tender age or judge me by my inexperience. I am the son of warrior Arjuna, with a gene pool of the great Pandavas and Krishna. While I was in my mother's womb, my father, who had recently learnt the formation of the chakravyuha from Guru Drona, was revising it in the chamber and explaining it to my mother.

'From inside the womb, I learnt from him the skill required to break and enter the chakravyuha. Before he could finish explaining the way out of the deadlock, Mother fell asleep, but I am certain I will still find the exit. Please give me this opportunity to serve my land. Allow me to go to the battlefield and make my lineage proud. I shall return after decimating the enemy and unfurl the flag of victory.'

Yudhishthira was moved by Abhimanyu's words, courage, and confidence. Besides, at the time, he was his only hope, and thus, he gave Abhimanyu permission to enter the battlefield. The news of Abhimanyu going to war made his wife, Uttara, daughter of King Virat, beam with pride. Entering the Mahabharata was Abhimanyu's dharma as a warrior, and supporting her husband in such a time was Uttara's duty as a wife. A Kshatriya writes his destiny and glory on the battlefield, and she had to let her husband write his.

Showing no signs of distress or insecurity, she dressed up in all her fineries to send off her beloved in high spirits. As tradition stated, she prepared the aarti thali with sindoor, akshata, diyas, roses, marigold flowers, prasad, and Ganga jal. When Abhimanyu appeared in front of her, dressed in his armour like a knight, her eyes welled up with tears of love and pride. Composing herself, she ran her hands over the metal plate sitting over his chest and hands as though infusing them with her strength, silently praying that they would do their job of protecting her husband's heart and limbs well.

Despite the veil that she drew upon the countenance to hide the pain of her conflicting emotions, Abhimanyu sensed her apprehension. 'Beautiful one! Don't let tears dim the sparkle of your eyes, for I want to capture that very spark and take it along with me to set alight the enemy's pyre.'

Uttara smiled as her heart was yet again filled with the warrior's fervour. Wiping her wet eyes, she applied vermilion on Abhimanyu's forehead and spoke, her tone assertive, 'Go and reduce them to dust. Bring back our pride. I shall await your return'.

Abhimanyu left, his chariot heaving with weapons, to meet his mother Subhadra and seek her blessings. As a Kshatriya woman, watching the men in her life go to the battlefield was something she had grown accustomed to over the years. Only a few days before, she had maintained a stoic stance as Arjuna left for the war. Now, however, her mind refused to accept the sight before her—her young son decked from head to toe in military gear and heading to the war.

This, her motherly heart could not bear. It overpowered easily all other duties she was obliged to fulfil as a Kshatriya queen. Her apprehension and worry showed clearly in her stooping posture, the wrinkles on her forehead, and the blinding sorrow in her eyes. 'Mother, why do you worry?' Abhimanyu held her hands tenderly. 'Do you not see in me the valour of my great father? Do you not have faith in me that I shall vanquish the enemy?'

Subhadra listened in silence as her teenage son tried to calm her, but nothing he said, no reason, no argument, however valid, soothed her. However, her duty as a queen reigned supreme, and she was compelled to push aside her fears. 'Go, my son. Go on now to Kurukshetra and lay to rest the enemy forever. Victory shall be yours!'

Abhimanyu raced towards the enemy line like the wind and cut into it, his arrows sparing none who came in the way of his chariot. Soon, he had entered the chakravyuha. The remaining Pandavas followed after him, as was the plan, but Jayadratha came between them and Abhimanyu. Yudhishthira, Bhima, Nakul, and Sahadeva together could not vanquish him for he was empowered by Lord Shiva's boon that he would be able to subdue the four Pandava brothers for a day.

The chakravyuha, by then, had closed behind Abhimanyu, and he kept moving further, slaughtering Kaurava warriors by the dozens. Yudhishthira, aware that his young nephew needed help, was growing anxious. Jayadratha was invincible. Moreover, neither of the four brothers knew how to break the chakravyuha, and thus, could not find another path to enter it.

Abhimanyu, isolated completely from the rest of his army, continued to inflict carnage until he reached the centre of the formation where some of the greatest warriors of the time awaited him—Dronacharya, Duryodhana, Dushasana, Ashwatthama, Kripacharya, Karna, and Shakuni, among others. He took them on one by one, defeating them in turn, rightly justifying his prodigious fame. So far, the Pandavas had dominated the war. The Kauravas were desperate to inflict a brutal blow, and this, they knew, was their opportunity. Ignoring the rules of the war that allowed only one-on-one battles between warriors, they attacked him at once.

The Kauravas killed Abhimanyu's charioteer and horses, and Karna broke his bow. Abhimanyu then drew his sword and shield, but they were also broken by Drona and Karna. Abhimanyu made the chariot wheel his weapon next, and that, too, met the same fate. Finally, he picked up a mace and, with it, razed the chariots of Ashwatthama and Dushasana's son. The latter then picked up a mace and duelled with Abhimanyu.

After several minutes of fighting, there came a point when the two struck each other senseless. While Abhimanyu, exhausted by several hours of fighting hitherto, remained unconscious, the Kaurava stood up and lay one final blow to his opponent, thus ending Abhimanyu's short but heroic life.

When Arjuna returned that evening and heard the news of Abhimanyu's death, it devastated him. Once he learnt about the chain of events leading to his son's death, Arjuna concluded that the person most responsible for his son's death was Jayadratha. Had it not been for him, Abhimanyu would have had his uncles by his side to fight with him, and consequently, he would have lived. Fuelled with rage, Arjuna vowed to kill Jayadratha by sunset the next day in Kurukshetra or end his own life by self-immolation. Everyone else who heard the news was shattered—his uncles, his mother Subhadra, Draupadi, and Krishna. This young boy had been the apple of everyone's eyes.

Most derived consolation from the knowledge that the adolescent had died fighting some of the greatest warriors of the generation and, in doing so, had become immortal. Whatever the outcome of the Mahabharata was, Abhimanyu's final battle and his courage would be remembered forever. However, nothing could console Uttara. After all, she was just a young girl. What was she to do now that her beloved had left her alone in this world? She knew the answer and rushed immediately to her elders.

'I, too, shall depart this planet to be with my partner, for what purpose will I serve here? He paid his dues to the motherland, and now I shall unite with him and leave this world too', she cried. All the elders were overcome with sorrow and pity. What could they possibly say to console this young girl who had lost her husband? What could they possibly do to make her change her mind?

It was then that Krishna set aside his pain and spoke, 'Child! Abhimanyu played his role and fulfilled his duties towards his family and motherland. He breathed his last while performing his karma, and now, it is your turn to do so. It is not time for you to think of departing, for you are carrying in your womb the future of the Pandavas' clan. You are Abhimanyu's beloved wife, and like him, it is your turn to become an epitome of courage.

'You have to give birth to this child and raise him by instilling in him all the qualities of a good ruler, for your son shall become the future king of this empire and torchbearer of this dynasty. He shall be the greatest king of all time, so, my child, remember your husband, be as brave as him, and fulfil your worldly duties.'

Uttara, unmoved by Krishna's words, continued to plea to the elders to let her perform the act of self-immolation. 'In your next birth in the Kali Yuga, you shall reunite with Abhimanyu and then fulfil your wish of leaving along with him from this world to the heavenly abode. You shall reap the fruits of your labour and courage in this life...you will be revered as a Devi, an epitome of a complete woman, and worshipped by thousands', Krishna blessed her.

Although still distraught, Krishna's words instilled in her a sense of purpose in life—her son. The war carried on, oblivious to the grief of the young widow—one among tens of thousands. She carried on too, in attire now stripped of all colour, much like her life. Her body no longer bore the ornaments they did once, and her skin no longer shone with its once youthful exuberance. She rarely spoke now or stepped out of her room, wounded too deeply by that last sight of her beloved husband shrouded in white. In one day, the fifteen-year-old princess of Matsya had become decades older. In one day, her unborn child had lost its father.

The soil of Kurukshetra had turned brick-red by now, stained forever with the blood of lakhs of warriors. Abhimanyu's death had turned the war even more gruesome. Neither side cared about dharma anymore—it was all about winning. To those whose loved ones had been killed on the battlefield, the war had long been lost. Uttara now looked like the shadow of her past self. Sleep was hard to come by. When it did, she would wake up at odd hours, body shaking uncontrollably, traumatised by the dreams of her beloved Abhimanyu losing his life on the battlefield. Then she would run her hand on the bed next to her and realise that it was no dream. Abhimanyu was no more. The truth would hit her with as much force as it did the first time she had heard it, and the cycle would repeat. Every day, she was widowed a hundred times over.

Through that haze of grief and agony, the young widow kept the promise she had made to herself and Govind. Her husband did not run away from the battlefield; he fought till his last breath. This was her battlefield now, and running away was not a choice. Perhaps the gods took pity on the young widow and many others like her and decided that the war had made humanity suffer enough. On the eighteenth day thus, the war finally came to its inevitable conclusion—with the victory of the Pandavas. However, Ashwatthama was still keen on revenge. Having killed all of the Pandavas' sons, he thought if he could kill the only remaining successor of Kuru Vansha, he would succeed in wiping out the Pandavas' lineage.

Meanwhile, Uttara lay on the bed in her chamber, listening absent-mindedly to the many occupants of the palace of Hastinapur. The Pandavas had finally emerged victorious in the war that had claimed her husband's life. She found no reason to rejoice. *I can't wait to see the throne with its rightful occupant...*Taatshri as king would be a sight to behold. She remembered his dream. *I can't wait to see the palace where father grew up...*what a blessed place that must be to have seen the births of the five greatest warriors of this generation.

She looked around her grand chamber, its opulence meaningless to her. *I will always be with you.* She bit her lips to confine the cry that tried to escape it. She looked then at her stomach, swollen and throbbing. All she wanted was a son who took after his father—brave and compassionate. Overcome by grief, she closed her eyes and sobbed quietly. Outside her chamber, the palace was gearing up to welcome the new king; aarti thalis were being prepared, garlands were being threaded, the throne and the crown were being polished, and a variety of delicacies were being cooked in the kitchen. Uttara remembered her late husband's words yet again.

Did the throne matter anymore, she thought bitterly, when it lay smeared with the blood and tears of millions? Suddenly, there was a knock on her door. With great difficulty, Uttara propped herself up on the bed and hastily wiped her eyes. In came Raajmaata Kunti and Queen Gandhari. 'Putri', said Kunti, placing her hand on her head, 'you are the sole reason we continue to live… our old ears cannot bear anymore the wails of widows that echo through this kingdom. Fill this palace with the cry of a baby soon. Give us a reason to smile and rejoice'.

Gandhari wiped her tears. 'This war has taken everything away from us. Your baby is the only future we have, Uttara.'

Later that night, bothered by a wave of anxiety and fear that would not let her sleep, Uttara started walking around the palace. Suddenly, the ground appeared to rumble. Uttara took a step back, hands covering her belly protectively. Her heart throbbed restlessly. Her instincts tingled. 'Maata? Raajmaata?' She looked around at the isolated hall.

Suddenly, a shadow sprang at her and in the silver moonlight, she saw its gleaming eyes. 'Guruputra Ashwatthama?' Terrified, she took a step back. Was he really there? Or was she imagining it? She barely had the time to react when a blinding light with a surging heat filled the room. Uttara stumbled backwards, screaming in pain as darkness engulfed her. She lost consciousness before she crashed on the floor.

Krishna was livid. 'You coward! You abomination! You targeted an unborn child with your *astra*...how dare you! You will pay heavily for this heinous act.' He ordered Ashwatthama to surrender the Mani in his forehead, which was the source of his godly strength and fearlessness. He further cursed Ashwatthama—'You will roam forests in complete isolation for an eternity. The wound in your forehead will never heal, and your body will become affected by a host of incurable diseases, forming sores and ulcers that bleed and ooze with puss. You will suffer in this state for thousands of years, hoping and pleading in every living moment for death to embrace you.'

When Uttara opened her eyes, she was in bed, surrounded by the entire Kuruvansh. Vaidyas ran around the room feverishly. Her mothers-in-law sat on the bed on either side of her. 'What happened? I was walking and suddenly...Ashwatthama attacked. Didn't my husband's blood satiate him?' Uttara yelled. Immediately, her tone changed, realising suddenly a singular horror. She ran her hands over her stomach and asked, 'Is my child...'

'Govind saved you both', said Panchali.

Uttara heaved a sigh of relief and closed her eyes momentarily to thank him. The next morning, she woke up in unbearable pain. All the women of the palace gathered in the chamber to see the birth of Abhimanyu's heir. Uttara suffered the pain in silence. To her, it was nothing compared to the pain she had endured after her husband's death. Finally, after a few hours, the baby was born. However, the chamber sat silent. Everyone was horrified—the child was dead. With her body drenched in sweat, Uttara stared coldly at the ceiling, unable to feel anything. Women in the chamber stifled their gasps.

Krishna walked into the chamber and picked up the infant. Immediately, wails of the new-born filled the air. Tears of joy ran down the cheeks of every person in the room; how many could claim to have watched Govind perform a miracle? Uttara took her baby in her arms and kissed him on the forehead.

'He took birth fighting difficulties—call him Parikshit', said Krishna.

Uttara watched her son intently. He had his father's nose. Wouldn't Abhimanyu be overwhelmed, just like her, with happiness and pride to see his son? Wouldn't he want to hold him, just like her, close to his chest to feel Parikshit's heartbeat against his? Wouldn't her heart swell with joy to see her beloved husband teach their son archery? Wouldn't life be perfect for their family of three, away from wars and bloodshed?

Tears rolled down Uttara's cheeks, and she hugged her son, making a promise to herself in that moment—she would raise her child the way Krishna had asked her to, a son worthy of carrying on the lineage of his brave father, a son worthy of being a king. Astrologers predicted a bright future for the kingdom and its heir. They predicted that Parikshit would usher in a new era in Hastinapur once he took over as the king. Celebrations broke out in the palace, lifting the dark veil of sadness that had covered its face hitherto.

As the baby gradually learnt the ways of life, so did the young mother. Every day, Uttara started learning again the things she had forgotten, things that brought joy, and she began allowing herself little moments of untamed bliss. After Abhimanyu's death, for a while, it had seemed as though life lost all meaning. Parikshit's arrival restored that imbalance. In him, she would see Abhimanyu. The boy was a splitting image of his late father. He not only resembled him, but his mannerisms were similar too. Parikshit's arrival changed not just his mother's world but those around her too.

The palace was a different place now than what it had been during the Mahabharata. Laughter and giggles saturated the air. Wounds began healing. Uttara was now the respected queen of Hastinapur and mother to the prince. Parikshit was loved by one and all. The toddler would often be found running around the lawn, chasing adults. Laughter became a habit in the palace. For the future king, training began early. With Kripacharya as his guru, he started learning the skills required for a Kshatriya—riding horses and practising archery. He would often come back with his tiny body covered in bruises, much to his mother's dismay.

It reminded Uttara of the days when Abhimanyu returned from training with his hands and feet blanketed in bruises. As she would treat his wounds, often with anger, Abhimanyu urged her to look at them not as bruises but as prizes, gleaming trophies of his hard work. Parikshit soothed his mother the same way, much to her chagrin. He was learning gradually about the gravity of his lineage and the legacy of his father. He often asked his mother about him, and she would put him to sleep with stories of Abhimanyu's short but remarkable life.

Before Uttara knew it, her little boy had grown up. He was ready to be crowned the king of Hastinapur. When the Pandavas left for *Mahaprasthan* after Krishna's death, Parikshit was crowned the king. One of the first things he did after ascending the throne was to put together a team of pandits and scholars from all over the kingdom to discover and write the Vedic texts that had been lost to time. He was praised by one and all and hailed as a revolutionary, for he was not just an exemplary warrior but a man of great wisdom and knowledge too. Thus, Uttara kept her promise. She gave Hastinapur its greatest king and, in doing so, fulfilled her dharma.

Masterji placed the scripture back and retired the class for the day. On the way back home, Narayani remained quiet, not conversing with Radha or Durga, her bestfriends-turned-classmates. Something latent buried inside her was stirred by Abhimanyu's and Uttara's story; she felt incapable of reigning in an inexplicable, restless energy. During the evening sadhana with her parents, failing to sit still, she got up to leave.

'Sit! Speak to Lord Narayan, he will calm you', said Gurshamal.

Narayani complied and sat down. She began questioning the lord, seeking answers for her restlessness. The Lord answered through her conscience, 'Your soul and purpose are connected. Wait for time to unfold the mystery. Do not be in a hurry; it will come to you when the time is right'.

That night in her dreams, she saw the war. She

watched humans fall on the edge of swords and perish. She watched the soil of Kurukshetra turn red, oblivious to the cries of those who watched their loved ones die. Even after she woke up the next morning, the horrors of the Mahabharata refused to leave her. In her mind, the story of Mahabharata played in circles giving birth to endless questions. Every day she would go to school with her bag full of books and a mind bursting with questions. She would bombard Masterji with questions, 'How can one be so courageous and principled at such a tender age? It seems impossible! And how could the elders allow it?'

'These qualities have little to do with age…they are placed in an individual by destiny and manifested by parents', answered Masterji.

'How could he not think about me? Not be concerned about my tender age, my love for him, and my desire to live my whole life with him and our child…was the Kshatriya dharma and debt of the motherland all that mattered to him?' Narayani spoke involuntarily, yet again in a trance, tears of rage and sorrow flowing from her eyes.

'Narayani?' Masterji patted her cheeks and gave her a glass of water.

Narayani looked at the glass in her hands, confused.

'Drink.'

She followed her teacher's instruction.

'Take deep breaths…'

'Masterji, why did he do it?'

'Narayani, humans who are chosen by destiny to

become legends—humans with a purpose higher than the ordinary man—have to lead a life confined to their purpose, they leave the *sood* (acknowledgment) of their body, relations, and other worldly attachments behind, for their purpose is of utmost priority. They are chosen to set examples, to create history, to display courage in the face of adversity and to live on long after they die. Abhimanyu fulfilled the duty assigned to him and only then departed the world, but Uttara's role as a mother was still unfulfilled. Her purpose, her duty demanded that she stay on the planet for a longer time.'

Narayani nodded, her burning questions finally answered. She experienced several fits and bouts of sorrow and rage as she learnt about the sequence that followed. Masterji explained then the bitter truth of life—it is unfair at times. In the end, when the entire Kuru Vansha was abolished, Masterji concluded, 'No one including God can ever escape the fruit of their karma. Every action has a reaction and repercussion irrespective of time and the age of its manifestation. Even Lord Krishna had to bear the brunt of a mother's curse…Gandhari cursed him for not stopping the war in spite of knowing the outcome prior. Her heart spewed out the curse after being compelled to witness the death of all her sons.'

While practicing with the sword later that day, Narayani was distracted. Noticing her inability to handle it, which was rather unusual for Narayani, Ghanshyam inquired, 'Narayani, what is wrong? Is this the first time that you've picked up a sword?'

Narayani put the sword back and came walking towards her teacher. Voice meek and head bowed, she said, 'These weapons of war bring death and sorrow to the world. It was these weapons that killed 1.66 billon people in Kurukshetra...lakhs of children were orphaned and women were widowed...what good does learning this skill do, *tau*? I...I don't want to learn it', she sobbed.

Overcome with pity, Ghanshyam's usual strict demeanour mellowed. Shedding his teacher's tone, he spoke in a fatherly voice, 'Beti, I can understand the pain you feel after learning the truth of life through one of humanity's darkest episodes in history. But your perception is blurred by emotions, my child. Think objectively and see, are all weapons used only to kill for selfish motives or power? No! Weapons can be used to save the world from falling into the wrong hands. Marred with ego and greed, when people forget their humanity, their diseased minds run the risk of spreading their infection in society.

In such times, the world demands the courage of those who still retain their humanity, to destroy the infected and bring about peace and balance. Narayani, creation and destruction work hand in hand to maintain the balance of the universe.'

Sparked by his words, she lifted the sword. 'I vow today to use my weapon only for the good of mankind. I promise *tau*!'

Ghanshyam smiled. 'I know you will. You have the war skills of an outstanding Kshatriya, the wisdom of a

Brahmin, the calculative mind of a Vaishnav, the work ethic of a Shudra, and above all, the heart of a rare, compassionate human. Bless you, my child!'

Narayani's education continued, her mind constantly irrigated with revolutionary ideas. Her questions never ceased; her outlook perpetually widened.

'Masterji! If Krishna was the Lord, the Almighty, the all-knowing, why did he let the war happen in the first place? Why didn't he use his magic and divine powers to restore peace?'

'I was waiting for this question from you, Narayani', said Masterji with a smile. 'When Gods descend to the planet, just like human beings, they are bound by the rules of the land. They perform their actions just like any other human so that they are relatable, so that they can set examples, become inspirations, and set milestones for the coming generations to reach, to follow and to abide by.'

Still not satisfied, she probed further, 'But Masterji, how can one justify the magnitude of cruelty and destruction to attain it? How can Gods be so merciless?'

'Every *yagna* demands a sacrifice, my child. For every breath you inhale, you have to let one out. This is the way to attain balance in nature. Thus, when gods descend to the earth, they have to follow this way of life. Even Gods bleed with tears of sorrow when watching their creation suffer, seeing the demise of those they themselves created. Yet again, karma is needed to restore dharma. And to fulfil their purpose assigned by destiny, they too have to sacrifice and suffer. So then, what is the lesson here for all of you?'

In chorus, the whole class repeated, 'We shall perform our karma as our dharma and shall never let our creator be appeased or ashamed of our deeds!'

Satisfied with their answer, Masterji smiled and dispersed the class for the day. From there, Narayani headed to the *akhara*.

'Where is *tau*?' She inquired once at the akhara. 'He isn't even in the *shastra shala*...'

With an audacious tone demanding authority, Ranjit answered, 'He is away with Durga and has asked me to lead the practice today. We will start with warm-up exercises as usual'.

Narayani did as told, running and exercising as they did every day before starting practice. She then brought the *bhaala*. Standing in an upright posture and holding it firmly before her, she bent her elbow and brought it parallel to her right eye. Holding her breath and steadying herself, she aimed at the target marked on the tree. Just as she pulled herself behind to release the throw, Ranjit spoke, 'Wait! Baba has asked to practice sword today, not *bhaala*. He has asked me to test you in a sword duel. Although I do not fight with girls and women, I cannot disobey him. Go bring your sword. If you are scared, you can back out...'

Smelling foul play but tied by the oath to never leave the battleground without putting up a fight, Narayani agreed to the duel. Ranjit was known in the entire taluka for his sword skills, he was unbeatable.

'Hail Lord Narayan!' Narayani lifted the sword with both hands and brought it to her head to pay reverence to the Gods and prayed for strength, focus, and victory. Assured of victory, Ranjit looked around with a smug look. It was only a matter of a few seconds before everyone around would clap after he had defeated Narayani. Watching him enter the akhara with his sword, everyone cheered him on, 'Ranjit! Ranjit!'

Narayani wiped the sweat off her brows and took a defending position.

'Please do not start crying if you lose…', he mocked her.

'Narayani, quit the duel. He will harm you; that seems to be his only intent', a tense Radha warned her friend. Narayani gave her a reassuring look and stood in position, observing her opponent's every movement carefully. With lightning speed, Ranjit placed his first blow on her sword. Overpowered with ease, the sword fell from Narayani's hands. Ranjit laughed uproariously and looked around, to see in the eyes of the spectators, appreciation and awe for his exemplary skills. By then, Narayani had picked up the sword. She stood now a little further away from him, one leg behind the other, and sword in front of her.

As he attacked her once again, Narayani bent on her hind leg, curved her back, and placed the sword horizontally across her face. Her move scattered the power of Ranjit's attack. Radha cheered wildly. Ranjit was surprised as were most of the spectators. Predicting his attack and defending it with such precision was not easy. Many before Narayani, with much more experience than her, had failed to do it. The fight continued. Although Narayani was on the defensive, it was evident that she was a worthy opponent.

Seeing little Narayani fight against the most renowned swordsman of the region for so long put to silence those who—until now—had been cheering for Ranjit. For nearly ten minutes, the silence was intervened only by the sounds of their swords dashing and spectators gasping. Narayani was as skilled at defence as Ranjit was in attack. However, Ranjit was tiring now. His moves lacked their initial power. Fearing defeat and unable to end the fight, he was growing restless.

Taking advantage of his diverted focus, Narayani placed an attack. Her powerful blow hit him hard and his sword fell to the ground. The crowd clapped. Ranjit looked around, seething in rage. The applause stopped instantly. Adamant to put an end to the fight, he picked up his sword and walked away to alight his horse tied nearby. Narayani looked on in disgust. He was cheating. She did not know how to ride a horse and the opponent had to be on the same ground.

He now began hovering above her. Taking advantage of the height, he placed blows on her from above. After defending herself twice, his third blow proved to be her undoing as she fell to the ground and the sword slipped several feet away from her. By this time, there was no strength left in her. She lay still, unable to move, every part of her body numb. Ranjit raised his sword.

'RANJIT! STOP!'

All eyes moved in the direction of the voice. It was Ghanshyam. He stood with his arms akimbo, eyes spewing fire. Blood drained from Ranjit's face on seeing him. He dismounted the horse immediately. The crowd dispersed and resumed practice. Radha rushed to Narayani's aid with water. 'Are you alright? You are crazy to have fought this animal. Couldn't you see that his intention from the beginning was to hurt you and not to teach?'

Ghanshyam, who had witnessed some of the fight, walked towards Narayani. 'You are a true fighter, *bitiya*! I am so proud of you! Your courage and grit are exceptional. I have not had a better student than you in several years of teaching. In the coming fair, you will represent my akhara in the fight.'

'But baba, I am—'

Ghanshyam cut him short, 'Ranjit, you better not utter a word. Skill alone does not make an exceptional warrior, humility does. Fighting is not just about skills, it is also about ethics and morals. Which you clearly have not learnt'.

Annoyed, Ranjit walked away. Just then, he saw Gurshamal emerge from behind a tree. He had been standing there and watching the entire scene unfold. His entire being oozed with rage. Fear and shame smeared all over Ranjit's face, his eyes did not meet Gurshamal's as he crossed him. It had been excruciating for Gurshamal to watch his daughter battle the brute. But he knew that by not helping her, he was preparing her for the battles that awaited her further in life. Her battles were hers, and however harsh the life lesson, she had to learn it. If he went now to console her, she would break down.

So, he turned around and started walking away. The scene of Ranjit seated on a horse hovering over his daughter kept playing in front of his eyes. Once he reached the crossroads, instead of turning right to go home, he headed the opposite way and stopped finally at a mansion—the home of a rich Muslim trader. He knocked on the door. A stout man with big brown eyes and a beard made orange by repeated application of henna opened the door.

'Gurshamal? Aren't you Gurshamal, the chilli trader?'

Gurshamal nodded.

'Please come in. Let me get you a glass of water, you are out of breath.'

Gurshamal sat down on the charpoy. The man returned soon with a steel glass and a jug full of water.

'It is rather hot outside…'

Gurshamal nodded and gulped down two glasses of water. He then spoke, 'I am aware that you supply horses to the Sultanate in Delhi…I want one too…the best breed of horse that you can find'.

'Don't mind me asking, what's your purpose behind buying a horse? You are a chilli trader, right?'

Gurshamal felt anger rising inside of him yet again. 'I want my daughter to learn horse riding. She will be representing the akhara in the coming state fair.'

'Queen Razia surely made an impact on the minds of people...this is impressive! A girl representing an akhara...she must be really good.'

'Yes, and she can be better.'

The Arab smiled. 'I shall bring the best breed for you...your daughter will fly on it.'

A week later, Narayani's training in horse riding began. The villagers, who by now had understood that gender norms did not apply to Narayani, were hardly surprised. In the coming days, just like every other skill she had mastered in a short time, Narayani learnt horse riding too.

She left everyone bewildered with her ability to mount a horse in one clean move. She rode fast and without the slightest fear. The wind appeared to bow down to her. It became usual for the villagers to see her riding her horse, running everyday errands. She would oblige children and the elderly with rides.

CHAPTER 9

The Daakin 🔱

One day, without prior notice, guests from Hisar arrived at Gurshamal's house.

'Laado, your baba has gone to attend the Panchayat meeting. Go inform him about the guests and ask him to return early, I will serve them snacks until then.'

Dressed in her baba's dhoti with a choli and a *dupatta* tied around the waist, Narayani mounted her horse and reached the Banyan tree within moments. As she made her way to the gathering, she heard the ongoing conversation of the Panchayat members.

'A *daakin* was spotted by many women and kids around the barren land adjacent to the neighbouring village. She kidnaps children and eats them. We have come to know that she speaks a different language and appears to talk to someone visible to no one but her. She is certainly not a human…it is our ill-fortune that she has now landed in our village. We need to do something… control this urgent situation before one of our children comes to harm. All members are requested to spread the message—no one should allow their children to go around that patch of land.'

'Laado, how come you are here? Is everything ok?' Gurshamal was surprised to see his daughter.

'Baba, there is a *daakin* in our village! That eats kids! How is it possible?' She asked, ignoring her father's question.

'Not of importance, just some rumours. Tell me, why are you here?' Shaken by his authoritative tone, she informed him about the guests waiting at home. 'You go home and help your mother, I will be there soon.'

Discarding the talks as rumours, Narayani rode back home humming songs and stopping at various houses on the way to pay her regards. Gurshamal followed soon, his thoughts occupied by news of the *daakin*. He was especially worried since that patch of land fell on the way to the *pathshala*. Many children walked that path every day. Aware of his daughter's inquisitive nature, he needed to dissuade her from taking the road. After having attended to the visitors, just as they were about to take leave, Gurshamal spoke in a loud voice, 'Bhaiya, while travelling back, avoid the patch of barren land connected to the adjacent village as it has been taken over by the Delhi Sultanate to fertilise it. They have sent a message to all villages to avoid using it'.

Hearing this, Narayani asked, 'That same land that the council was talking about, baba? The one where the *daakin* lives?'

The guests were surprised.

'*Daakin*?' Gurshamal let out a laugh. 'They are just rumours to keep kids away. There is no *daakin*.'

The next morning, singing the *Vishnu Sahasranama*, Narayani headed to school. Lost in her song, she forgot her father's instructions entirely and ended up taking her usual route to her *pathshala*. Humming while kicking a pebble, the isolation of her surroundings evaded her notice. 'Narayani! Narayani!'

She heard Radha call her from behind. Just as she was about to turn around, she saw in the distance the silhouette of a tall, fat figure. By then, Radha stood right beside her. She grabbed her hand and pulled hard.

'Have you gone mad? Don't you know what everyone says? There is a *daakin* in this area who kidnaps and eats kids. Now let's hurry and get out of here before she catches us.'

Radha held her hand and began to run. It took Narayani a minute to realise that the fat, tall figure might have been that of the *daakin*. She turned around but she was no longer there.

'Did you see something?'

'See what?' Radha asked, trying to catch her breath.

'That…', Narayani turned around yet again to see the vast, empty land.

Dismissing it as an illusion, she started running faster to catch up with her friend.

'You are too slow! Whoever reaches the *pathshala* last is a donkey!'

Later that evening at the temple, Narayani was gorging on her favourite prasad when she noticed Bholu standing between his parents with his head hanging low. Determined to cheer him up, she ran to him and offered some *boondi*.

'You like this, right? Here, have some more.'

He shook his head and stood still, refusing to make eye contact with her. Narayani felt concerned, for Bholu was always in high spirits. Once his parents went to speak to Panditji, Narayani stepped closer to him and put her hand on his shoulder.

'What is the matter, Bholu? You can tell me. I promise I will not tell anyone. Did someone bully you? Tell me, I will punch that person hard.' He looked up at her with tears in his eyes.

'I saw the *daakin*. She is huge and fat. When she laughs, her broken, stained teeth become visible.'

'Did she hurt you? Is that why you are so upset?'

He shook his head. 'With her arms stretched, she was calling out to me…I started running and kept running till I could no longer hear her voice. Don't tell anyone, they will scold me for going there.'

She assured him and left, her mind now racing. There was definitely some truth to the *daakin* story that her father and other elders were hiding, she knew now for certain. She decided to find out the truth.

The next day, she carried some *jamuns* in her bag. While Masterji was away, she shared them with all her classmates. Once everyone was in high spirits, she made a proposition.

'It's the month of *Saawan* and after so many days, it is nice and cool. Let's go and swing on the big tree on our way back today.'

Relishing the *jamuns*, everyone agreed. After school, together they walked out, humming songs of rain. Narayani ran and reached the Neem tree with the swing first.

'Come Radha, give me a good push', she said. Radha pushed the swing and it started moving to and fro.

'Push harder, Radha!' Radha did as told. Narayani flew higher and higher with every push. She could now see far and wide. She was running her eyes in all directions, hoping to spot the figure that had tormented Bholu. Narayani's vigilant eyes kept scanning the area for a long time but no one appeared in sight.

'We should go now', said Meera, 'it's getting late.' She appeared nervous and tense.

'We are not allowed to be here. Let's rush back before anyone knows.'

'It is my turn to swing!' Dev cried.

'Don't worry, Dev, tomorrow we will come again, I promise! Right now, it's getting late, we can't let the elders get suspicious. If they find out, we will never be allowed to play here again.'

'Yes, true. We can't let them know.'

'This is our secret, not to be shared with any elder, agreed?' Narayani said.

'Yes!'

'I promise I won't tell anyone…'

'Yes, I want to come back tomorrow.'

Disappointed that the day's investigation had yielded no clues about the *daakin*, and knowing that their visits to the area were numbered, Narayani wanted to move fast. She went over all the facts that she knew—the *daakin* was not built like a normal human being. She was built like a demon, with a massive body, long nails, and crooked teeth, and she spoke in an incomprehensible language. She very likely had the strength of a demon and could not be overpowered by normal physical means. She concluded, based on these facts, that it would be impossible for her to fight the *daakin* with weapons or martial skills. She would have to resort to a more effective, smarter method.

'Laado! Laado!'

Narayani walked over to her father with a *lota* of water and inquired, 'What's in this packet, baba?'

Handing the bag to her, he said, 'Your mother had asked me to buy chillies for Lila. Go and give it to them. Make sure you wash your hands later or else your eyes will burn if you touch them by mistake.'

Almost instantly, Narayani had a plan. While her parents were seated in sadhana, she made a *potli* of chilli powder and hid it in her bag. The next morning in her *pathshala*, she proposed, 'Masterji! We have completed our task for today, can we go early as it is getting cloudy and might rain.' She turned around and winked at her classmates.

'Yes Masterji, can we please leave early today?'

Masterji nodded his head to collective jubilation from the class. They all rushed out of the classroom together, bubbling with joy. Meanwhile, Narayani took the chilli potli and hid it under her *odhani*, tucking it in her *ghaghra*'s belt. She then uttered a silent prayer, 'Narayan, please help me face the *daakin* and resolve this problem for everyone'.

Dev took the first turn on the swing. Narayani had her eyes on the distant horizon all around her. Except for Narayani and her friends, there was no one on that vast stretch of land. Once Dev finished his turn, Narayani grabbed the swing and stood on it to see further. As she began swinging, she spotted that silhouette she had seen for the first time a few days back. It was no illusion, she knew now. It was walking in their direction.

Although her heart was pounding, she kept her spirits up, not wanting to alarm or scare any of her friends. She started singing songs of rain loudly and her friends soon joined in. This attracted the *daakin* further and she moved towards them with swifter steps. At this point, Narayani did not want any of her friends to have the slightest idea that the *daakin* was walking towards them. She feared that the woman might be compelled to use some kind of supernatural powers and hurt them. She kept swinging, keeping an eye on her movement.

'Narayani, why is it that only you swing every day? We all should get a chance too!'

'You will all have your turns, be patient', she said.

The *daakin* looked like a hag with a huge frame. Hearing their song and laughter, she had increased her pace and was approaching them with arms stretched, thumping forward with a crooked posture. Her heart and mind racing, Narayani knew that she had to make her move at the right time; too quick or too late, and their lives could be in danger. Narayani could now see the tattered clothes and the layer of filth covering her body and hair. Her face was so thickly caked in mud that other than the whites of her eyes, nothing else was visible. Her chapped lips would part frequently to reveal her broken teeth.

'Run! Run! The *daakin* is here, she will eat us all', Bholu screamed.

'Run!'

Panic broke out and the children started running towards the village. Narayani's heart was thumping, her ears full of her friend's hysterical screams—'Run! Run!'

'Narayani, what are you doing? Come fast, COME!'

Her friends' voices now fading, Narayani got down from the swing, her legs trembling—a part of her wanted to run. She stood frozen between her friends, now beyond her reach, and the *daakin*, only a few feet away. She could hear the woman's voice now, a jumble of words she could not make any sense of, her arms spread wide as she walked towards Narayani. In that instant, only fear reigned supreme and Narayani lifted her *ghaghra* to run.

Just then, her hand touched the chilli *potli* she had prepared the day before. Taking a deep breath, she gathered all her courage, reached inside her *odhani* and pulled it out. She then filled her fist with powdered chilli and ran towards the *daakin*. Now at an arm's length from her, with precision and swiftness, Narayani jumped high, opened her fist and blew air so that the powdered chilli went straight into the *daakin's* eyes. The burn of the chilli made the *daakin* stumble backwards, howling in pain as she rubbed her eyes. She moved around disoriented, screaming, shouting and walking like a drunkard.

'Water! Water! Please help me! PLEASE!'

Narayani watched her from a distance, prepared for any further attacks from her but the *daakin* continued to scream and rub her eyes. Unable to bear the pain, she fell to the ground. Seeing her in a vulnerable position, Narayani stepped forward.

'You *daakin*! You eat kids. You were here to kidnap us and eat us. Do you have no conscience, you animal?'

The *daakin* rolled on the ground helplessly. She held Narayani's legs. 'Help me, please! PLEASE!'

Narayani winced in pain as the *daakin's* long nails dug into her flesh and drew blood. Narayani stepped back. Enraged, she picked up a massive rock from the vicinity.

'You will not hurt any child henceforth!' She said, holding the rock above her head, ready to strike.

'Don't kill me! Please don't! I am not a *daakin*. I don't eat kids. I am alone, I have no family. I love children. I could never harm a child...' Sobbing, she fell unconscious. Narayani looked at her, ridden with guilt. What if she was telling the truth? Hesitantly, she sat down beside her and parted her hair, ready to leap back should it be a trick employed by the *daakin* to trap Narayani. She could see now the many wrinkles on her old face. From up close, she appeared human, not like an evil *daakin*, as described by the elders in their stories.

Pity and guilt rose in Narayani's heart at once, realising her folly of having judged and acted based on hearsay alone. She went back to the swing to fetch her *jhola*. She extracted her water bottle from it and started sprinkling water in the *daakin*'s eyes. The *daakin* lay unconscious. Narayani was alarmed. Had she killed an old, helpless lady? Narayani kept pouring water into her eyes till all of the red chilli powder ran down the side of her face. The *daakin* came to her senses gradually. Narayani stumbled backwards, alarmed.

'Thank you! Thank you! Can you please give me some water to drink?'

'Yes, I will…' The *daakin* opened her mouth and just as Narayani had poured some water in it, she heard a mob approaching from behind her.

'Ae *daakin*, stay away from the child!'

'Kill her!'

'Narayani, step away from her!'

Narayani turned around to see the entire village walking towards her, led by her father and Radha. Many men held *bhaalas* and swords in their hands. 'No, don't kill her…' Narayani got up and started walking towards them. 'Baba, she is not…'

Ganga came running towards Narayani and hugged her. 'Are you ok, Laado? Did she hit you?'

'She is bleeding from her leg.'

'Did the *daakin* do it?'

'No, no.' Narayani turned around to see the *daakin*. She was unconscious.

'Did you kill her?'

'No, she is breathing…'

'She is so ugly!'

'Laado, have you gone mad?' Ganga said, shaking her daughter by the arms. 'How could you even think of fighting that *daakin*? I have had enough of all this… getting educated and learning all these martial skills has bloated your little head. You will not step out of the house from today. What if something had happened to you? How would we live?'

'Now that she is unconscious, it is a good time to put an end to this danger looming over our village.'

'NO!' Narayani said. Freeing herself from her mother's grip, she wedged herself between the *daakin* and the village.

'LAADO, ENOUGH!' Her father thundered.

Although taken aback by her father's angry tone, Narayani did not budge.

'Baba, she is not a *daakin* who eats kids, she is a lonely, old woman with no family, seeking company. She is lonely, baba. She told me all this before she fell unconscious…she didn't once try to harm or attack me. It's only because of her looks that people feel this way…

she is just misunderstood…'

'Enough, Laado! You think all the elders are fools and you are the only clever one?'

'Ma, I…' Before she could finish her sentence, Ganga slapped her daughter. Narayani was stunned into silence. Neither of her parents had ever hit her before. Ganga then grabbed Narayani's hand and dragged her home. 'Baba…she needs help…she speaks like us…please listen to her once …' she cried as her mother dragged her away.

'All the women, please go back to your homes, let the menfolk see what is to be done with this *daakin*.'

Later in the evening, Gurshamal returned home. 'Narayani? Narayani?'

Ganga came into the living room.

'What happened to the *daakin*?'

'Where is Narayani?' Gurshamal asked.

'I have locked her in the room as punishment. That should teach her a lesson.'

Without uttering a word, Gurshamal opened the locked door. Narayani came running towards him, tears flowing down her cheeks. 'Baba, did you all kill her?'

'What a stubborn girl! She has still not learnt her lesson!' Ganga grit her teeth in anger.

'Calm down, Ganga. Our daughter was right. The *daakin* is a harmless lady.' Gurshamal seated Narayani on the charpoy and wiped her tears. 'Laado, she is alive. I did speak to her and not once did she attack or harm anyone. I knew then that we were all wrong about her. After some enquiries in the nearby villages, we learnt that she once had a family—a baby and a husband. One day, because of an unintentional mistake committed by her, her son died. Her husband and his family blamed her, called her a witch and had her thrown out of the village.

'She started living alone in a hut. That hut has drawings of a family, of a kid, of happy and sad times; her mental balance was obviously disturbed because of the nature of events. I have requested the Sarpanchji to allow her to stay in our village. *Vaidji* is treating her. My child, you were right.'

'Thank you for saving her, baba!' Narayani hugged her father.

'I am proud of you, Laado, only you had the wisdom to see beyond the obvious and get to the truth. If not for you, we all would have committed a sin today. May you forever walk the path of Truth.'

CHAPTER 10

Gangour Worship

Narayani ran the tip of her index finger, which was smeared with *kajal,* on the lower waterline of her almond-shaped eyes with deft precision.

'You look as gorgeous as maa and Mata Parvati', Narayani spoke to her reflection with pride. 'All the girls are going to envy you today. And Mata Parvati is surely going to bless you with a wonderful married life.'

Hidden from her daughter's view, Ganga listened to Narayani and smiled. Unable to hold herself back, she emerged from her hideout. '*Are*! *Are* wait! Let me apply the *kajal tikka* to shield my fairy princess from evil eyes.'

Startled then embarrassed as she realised her mother had heard her, Narayani's cheeks turned red.

'Maa...which *odhani* will match my red *ghaghra*?'

Ganga's eyes picked up the bright red one without even scanning the two other choices. 'This one. Even if I picked out another, this is the one you will want to wear.'

Narayani smiled.

'I know my daughter's taste very well', said Ganga, cupping her daughter's chin in her hand.

'I should go now, maa. I have to pick flowers on the way too...my Gangour will be the best dressed today, everyone else's will pale in comparison...'

Maiden girls and married women perform the Gangour *puja* to seek blessings from Mata Parvati, the Goddess of marital fidelity. With ashes collected from the auspicious fire of Holi, they mould deities of Gangour; *Gana*, a synonym for Lord Shiva, and *Gaur* for *Gauri* or Parvati symbolising *saubhagya* (marital bliss). Unmarried women pray to be blessed with a good husband and married women for welfare, health, long lives for their husbands, and a happy married life.

Ganga put a *kajal tikka* behind her daughter's ear then circled her palms over Narayani's head and pressed them on her temples to rid her of any ominous energy. She then watched her daughter walk out of the house with a spring in her step, humming and giggling, engrossed in her world of make-believe, and thought with bittersweet pain of the day when Narayani would step out of their house one final time, never to look back, to make another house her home.

Adorned in fineries, hands dyed with intricate patterns in henna, the eight girls, divided into groups of four, placed their Gangour under the shade of the big banyan tree that had overlooked the village for as long as the village had been.

*'Khol aye khol mata khol kiwaadi, baayi ubhi rowa
pujan wali'*, they sang in unison.
(Gangour Goddess, please open the door, we are
standing outside to offer our prayers.)

The Gangour puja began with them taking turns
to adorn their deities with *kajal* and vermillion *tikkas*,
offering sweets and narrating and reading together the
story of Lord Shiva and Mata Parvati.

'Look, Sheila, this year I have moulded my Gangour
with clay and not soil...it is so soft, isn't it? I stitched the
clothes with velvet and made the jewellery with beads
and stones from the Arab trader's shop. This year my
Gangour is the best, isn't it? Next year, you will have to
try very hard to outdo me!'

'I will not be here next year, Narayani...'

'What? Why?'

'I am getting married next month.'

'What!'

Narayani looked into her friend's eyes to see the
sadness she heard in her voice.

'Narayani, see the colour of your henna, it is so dark!
Your husband will love you more than Lord Shiva loved
Parvati. And your Gangour's beauty is so mesmerising...
you are surely going to be blessed with marriage soon.
Get ready to be a bride', teased Rukmani.

Sheila chuckled.

Narayani pushed her elbow into Rukmani's ribs. Imitating
her mother, Narayani put a *kajal tikka* on her Gangour.

'I am not marrying now or anytime in the near future. But it seems that you have already found your groom.'

The girls worshipped, laughed, and made merry, pulling each other's legs and admiring the design and colour of henna on each other's hands.

'Gor gor Ganpati, iswar puje Parvati, Parvati ka aalaa gila, gor ka sona ka teeka, de tamka de, bala rani vart karyo, khero khato laadu diyo…rani puje raj ne, me puja suhag ne, rani ko raj tapto jaaye, maharo suhaag badhto jaye.'

(Everyone worships the goddess, even Ganpati. May the goddess bless the queen with an ever-growing empire and me with marital bliss till eternity.)

The girls sang one final time. After a long puja on an empty stomach, it was time to worship a different god, the one in their stomachs. It was time to head home.

Narayani stayed behind to clear the offerings and collect her Gangour. While she was at it, she saw Sheila lost in thoughts and picked up the thread of conversation they had left a while ago.

'Sheila, you don't seem happy at all today…and you don't sound happy about your marriage either. Is everything alright? You can tell me what is in your heart. Maa says it's always good to speak out one's worries; if not, they become toxic.'

Sheila smiled. 'Your heart is as beautiful as your face…I am not sad, just apprehensive about the future. I trust my parents' decision and I know how much they love me...but something about marrying a person I haven't even seen, who is fifteen years older than me, doesn't feel right. This is not what I asked for year after year while performing this puja.'

She fell silent. Narayani stared at her Gangour, unable to find the right words to console her friend. Was there even consolation she could offer, she wondered. Just hearing Sheila talk about her groom sent a shiver down her spine. The idea of marrying a much older stranger was horrifying to hear, and this very idea was about to become her friend's reality.

Sheila bowed before the deities.

'I think I am worrying too much...this has always been the tradition...our parents know best and surely they would make the right choice for us. Besides, how does age matter? Like so many others, I am sure my married life will be successful too', she said, her tone barely convincing.

Narayani looked at Sheila, her eyes conveying her trepidation.

'I am sure Mata Parvati will give me a blissful married life. Look, I am happy and smiling. You were right, it does feel good to confide in you. Thank you so much for listening. I feel a lot better now. And yes, start preparing for my wedding.'

Although not convinced, Narayani forced a smile.

'My Gangour was the best, maa', Narayani declared, stepping into the house.

Ganga sat on the floor chopping vegetables. 'It had

to be. You worked hard to make the Gangour and your devotion surpasses every mortal I know. You must be hungry…there is kheer next to the *chulha*. Don't keep it waiting for too long.'

Narayani nodded and walked away. Ganga looked on, surprised. On any other day, Narayani would storm into the kitchen disregarding her mother's warnings not to. As the day rolled on, she noticed her daughter was not her usual self. The usual spring in her step was missing. Even when she fed Juggli, she appeared lost in her thoughts.

'Laado, come here.'

Narayani walked into the kitchen.

'Come here', said Ganga and seated her in her lap. 'Won't my Laado tell maa what's bothering her little heart?'

'Maa, how can a girl just leave her home after marriage and start an entirely new life with a stranger in a different home? We all choose what to wear, what to eat, but to marry, the girl has to accept a choice made by others. Why?'

Just then, Gurshamal walked in. 'What are maa and beti gossiping about?'

'We are talking about the Gangour puja celebrations today…how was your day?' Ganga said.

The conversation picked up a different thread as Gurshamal told his wife and daughter about the upcoming fair at Pushkar. Her spirits cheered by the prospect of a family trip, Narayani forgot about her worries. Life resumed as usual.

***

'The Pushkar Fair is scheduled next month', said Ghanshyam, running his finger on the blade of a sword, 'And as was decided earlier, Narayani will represent our *akhara* this year'. He looked at Narayani, chest bloating with pride.

Everyone burst into applause. Narayani stepped forward, her hands joined and her head bowed.

'Ghanshyam *tau*, thank you so much for your trust and for this opportunity. But I want to withdraw, please do not be offended by my decision. Let Ranjit *bhaiya* take my place in representing the *akhara*. He is a lot more experienced than me and a better contender. Besides, I had promised to use my martial skills and weapons for defence, not to win glory and awards.'

Ghanshyam put down the sword and walked over to her. Placing his hands over her head, he spoke, 'You are a true warrior, Narayani. You understand the real use of a shield and a sword. Your conviction is absolutely remarkable…even glory failed to dissuade you from your chosen path. I am so proud of you!'

Ghanshyam looked at Ranjit and nodded his head. Ranjit took a step forward towards Narayani and apologised to her. Narayani extended her hand towards him.

'*Bhaiya*, I will forgive you only if you bring us the title of 'Best *Akhara*' this year like you do every year.'

He ran a hand over her head. 'I promise, *behen*! This year too, our *akhara* shall win the title. *Jai Bhavani!*

CHAPTER 11

Hisar

Kamal Ram followed Tandhan like a tail as the latter paced nervously in the corridor.

'Stop! Listen, when baba comes, we will see his mood and if it's any good, then we put forward our demand.'

'Hmm, ok.'

Jaliram stepped into the corridor.

'Where are you two going at this hour? Have you both finished your practice of accounts?' He asked.

Startled, Tandhan turned around. 'No baba, we are not going anywhere. We finished our day's practice. We were waiting for you.'

Kamal Ram took his father's *jhola* and, along with his brother, followed Jaliram into the living room. Yamuna came in with a *lota* of water. Tandhan took it from her and offered it to Jaliram. 'You must be tired and thirsty after the long walk from the Nawab's palace, baba. Here, have some water.'

Kamal Ram began fanning his father as the latter took a sip. This kind of hospitality from the brothers was unusual. Yamuna and Jaliram exchanged a look.

'Now, enough of buttering, what do you both want?'

Embarrassed, Tandhan spoke, 'Baba, when we were in Delhi, you always attended the annual Pushkar Fair and returned with goodies and stories about the gathering... the variety of goods that the traders put up, the sale of animals, the competitions among akharas from various villages, the display of cultural art and skills...the Pushkar Fair has always fascinated us. We both have always wished to attend it but the distance made it inconvenient. Now that we have moved to Hisar, which is relatively closer, can you please let us come with you?'

'Yes baba, please let us come. Please!' Kamal Ram said.

Jaliram looked at Yamuna and she nodded.

'Ok! Ok! You both can come along. It will be a good learning experience for you. Now come, let's have dinner, I am starving.'

The three sat down for dinner. Yamuna started serving hot chapattis from the *chulha*. After a quick thanksgiving prayer to goddess Annapurna, Tandhan and Kamal Ram fed their mother the first bite as was a ritual for the brothers.

'All the love only for your mother', said Jaliram and laughed.

As they all started eating, Jaliram shared the day's events at the court of Nawab Jhadchand and how the administrative policies were successively bringing prosperity to the district of Hisar.

'Today at the market while I was buying vegetables, I overheard the sellers speak', said Yamuna, 'Jaliramji is a very good *Diwan*. In such a short duration as the administrative head, he has been able to give us better roads to travel...saves us so much time and saves our goods from perishing. He is an exceptional administrator. Hisar is soon going to prosper and outdo all other districts. Your hard work is being appreciated by one and all. You have won a lot of hearts.'

'Yes baba, even at the school and the *akhara*, I hear people praising your policies...they say that they are beneficial to both the law and the people', said Tandhan.

'Baba's efficiency is unprecedented...no wonder the Nawab of Hisar sent his courtesan to Delhi and offered baba the post of *diwan*.'

'You all have fed me enough praise for a month at least, leave some room for the food.' Jaliram laughed. 'It is my duty to serve people to the best of my ability...and with Lord Shiva's blessings with me, I am bound to be successful.'

Tandhan and Kamal Ram began preparations for the Pushkar Fair. They started saving money more diligently than ever.

'Kamal, my wish to buy a horse that flies like an eagle might get fulfilled there. If I find a horse that matches the one in my dreams, I will request baba and use my savings to buy it. Do you think he will allow us?' Tandhan asked as they walked down the road.

'Yes, *bhaiya*! I am sure baba will not refuse…I will give you my savings too. Will you let me ride it then?'

Tandhan laughed. 'Even if you don't, I will still teach you and let you ride it. As long as you take care of it and are responsible, it will be our horse and not just mine.'

'Tandhan! Kamal! Wait for me!'

Panting, Raj Kumar, the son of the Nawab, caught up with them.

'I heard you are attending the Pushkar Fair?'

'You heard right!'

'Oh! I wish I could come along but *Abbu* won't allow it. He says it's not a place for me to visit. It's a place for villagers and sellers, not for royalty…bring me something exquisite, please? I shall pay you the amount.'

Ignoring his condescending remark about common villagers and his pompous show of heritage, they replied, 'Yes Raj Kumar, we surely will. Now let's play a game of throwball and see the power of your royal blood!'

By then, the boys had reached the wasteland that was used as a playground by the children of the village. The game began. One by one, the boys took turns throwing the ball highest and furthest. It was Raj Kumar's turn.

'Kamal, go fetch the ball', he said after throwing the ball.

'This is not a court, Raj Kumar, we are all friends here, all equal. Please go and bring the ball yourself, my friend,' said Tandhan.

His stern but polite tone conveyed the message without being disrespectful. Like his father, Tandhan was popular among his friends for his ability to balance diplomacy and righteousness. At the *akhara*, he often lost duels to amateurs on purpose to boost their confidence. In spite of being the best swordfighter and wrestler in his *akhara*, the only time he put his skills to use was against an arrogant opponent. His tall and lean stature had earned him a considerable following from the opposite sex. They would find silly excuses to talk to him and get his attention, 'Excuse me, can you please help me pull a bucket of water from the well?' Kamal, who was often accompanying his brother whose response to such queries was always a cold shrug, would offer a different deal.

'Why trouble *bhaiya* when I am here to serve you?'

One day, on their way back from school, the brothers decided to take a short break. Along with their friend, Shyam, they stationed themselves on a luscious green field.

'Tandhan,' said Shyam, playing with a blade of grass, 'who is going to be your bride from this village? I have seen your image in the eyes of girls who follow you everywhere. I have heard your name in the prayers of their mothers. I have seen pride and envy in the eyes of men when they see you. But you, my friend, whose image do you carry in your eyes?'

'*Bhaiya* knows about the horse he wants, not the girl he wants to marry', said Kamal.

Tandhan rolled his eyes.

'Who will be the lucky girl who will hold your hand and put a garland around your neck?' Shyam prompted.

Tandhan looked towards the horizon where green fields merged with the blue sky and said, 'No one has appealed to my heart yet or won my attention. I don't know who will walk beside me hand in hand. All I know is that she will be a very special girl'.

Disappointed by his response, Shyam teased him. Tandhan remained lost in a dream-like state, oblivious to his friend's taunts, thinking about that day when he would meet the girl of his dreams.

'*Bhaiya*, enough dreaming, let's rush home, we have to start packing for the trip.'

The brothers got up and ran home after a hurried goodbye to Shyam. The moment they pushed open the door of their house and stepped inside, huffing and panting, they were met with the angst-ridden face of their father.

'What's the matter, *baba*? You look tense, is everything alright at the court?'

Still pacing across the room, Jaliram answered, 'Your trip to Pushkar Fair has to be cancelled. The Nawabs from Delhi are visiting the court for inspection and discussion. My presence is mandatory. I will not be able to attend the fair, boys. I am so sorry, the circumstances are not in my control'.

Tandhan and Kamal let out a collective sigh. Later that night, dinner was accompanied by silence and gloom. Yamuna tried to console them with a promise to buy new clothes but in vain.

'I will be back in a while', said Jaliram after finishing dinner and heading out.

Resting his head in Yamuna's lap, Kamal vented his frustration. 'Why does *baba* have to take up all responsibilities, *maa*? Can't he just come? Surely there are others who can manage the visitors...'

'*Baba* is the most loyal and intelligent person in the court. Nawab Jhadchand depends on him completely. It's ok...I am sure Lord Shiva has better plans for us', said Tandhan, no inkling of disappointment on his face.

Kamal got up with a jump. 'No amount of explanation is going to console me, *bhaiya*. I am going to tell *baba* tomorrow that he is unfair.'

Distancing his *charpoy* from his father's, Kamal drew the white sheet over his head and dozed off sulking.

The next day, the brothers' sour mood remained as they went to the *akhara*.

'Have the two of you received a spanking at home or have you not been given food to eat? What's the matter with you two?' Ranaji said. He picked up a *lathi* and looked at Tandhan. 'Let me see you perform all the defence and attack moves that I have taught you. Keep your problems aside and practice with utmost focus. No problem should be an obstacle during practice.'

With infallible precision, Tandhan put up a performance of ten defence and seven attack moves in fifteen minutes. Everyone broke into applause as he concluded his performance.

'Your moves are so swift and clean, it's like watching a dancer perform!' Ranaji said.

There were days when Tandhan managed to beat him too, the very teacher who had taught him everything he knew. Wiping his sweat and gulping a whole glass of buttermilk, Ranaji summoned Tandhan and Kamal Ram.

'Now, tell me what the matter is. Why do my handsome nephews have frowns on their faces?'

'We were to attend the Pushkar Fair with *baba* this year. But due to some urgent work commitments at court, our trip has been cancelled. All our preparations and dreams wasted', said Kamal.

'Here, have a drink.' He offered a glass of buttermilk to both. 'Well...I can take permission from *Diwan* Jaliram ji and take you both along with me. He trusts me and I am sure he won't say no.'

Tandhan and Kamal nearly dropped their glasses of buttermilk.

'Will you, Ranaji?' They asked in unison.

'Yes.'

Later that night at dinner, Kamal couldn't stop fidgeting and shifting around restlessly.

'What's the matter with you, Kamal? Sit still!' Yamuna said and looked at her husband with a bemused look on her face.

'I know what will make him sit still, Yamuna', said Jaliram.

Kamal looked at his father, confusion and curiosity writ large on his face.

Jaliram heaved a sigh and put his morsel down. 'You two can attend the fair with Ranaji. After all, he is family', he said.

Ranaji was a Rajput who headed the infantry at the court of Nawab Jhadchand. His warfare skills, loyalty, and courage had earned him widespread popularity and respect. Owing to similarities in their work ethic, Jaliram and Ranaji had become friends and, eventually, family. A staunch Rajput, Ranaji had no family of his own. He had lost his wife and only sister in an attack by Mughal invaders. The incident had both toughened and soured him. His demeanour softened only for Jaliram and his family. He had started training Kamal and Tandhan on Diwan Jaliram's request and, as days passed, he become more of an uncle to the boys than their coach.

He instilled in them qualities of courage and loyalty. When he found them steering away from the path set by him, he was quick to reprimand them, but just as easily he would spoil them when he thought they deserved it. Aware of Tandhan's fondness for horses, he allowed him to ride his horse. After clearing his tests for sword fighting and wrestling, Tandhan would ask, 'Ranaji, my reward?' In reply, Ranaji would let him ride his horse.

He was not a staunch fighter in that he valued diplomacy too.

'Not all battles are won with weapons. Always take a calm, logical look at the situation and then decide if it needs your hands or words. Even diplomacy is a way of fighting battles', he would always tell them.

'Just like you favour the villagers even while serving Mughals!' Tandhan would retort.

Soon, the big day arrived.

'I have packed enough food to last for two days. Kamal, make sure you share with Ranaji and Tandhan as well, it's not for you alone', said Yamuna. 'Do not gorge too much on sweets or other food or you will end up with an upset stomach. Stay close to them, don't wander around on your own.'

'Yes, *maa*! I am the naughty and undisciplined one, Tandhan never creates any problems. He is your favourite, your only good son!' Kamal sulked.

Tandhan pulled him close. 'Enough drama, now get ready for the fun!' He whispered in his ear.

After receiving their parents' blessings, the boys mounted the cart already filled with other villagers. Behind them, half a dozen caravans with livestock and goods waited for them to move. Tandhan and Kamal were ecstatic and the wind appeared to mirror their mood. The zeal in their hearts danced to the tunes of the songs that women in the carts behind them sang. Aware yet oblivious to the affectionate stares he received from the *jananis* every time the *purdah* of their bullock cart flew open, Tandhan was cherishing every moment of the journey. The happy rhythm of the moving cart was in tune with his body and his thoughts were filled with the promise of a massive, colourful gathering with a show of skills, culture, goods, and fineries. He could not wait to get there.

Since the journey was long, the men took turns to sit and walk. Kamal walked fast enough to remain aligned with the cart full of young girls.

'Kamal, walk fast!' Tandhan would yell at his brother.

'Yes, yes, *bhaiya*! Coming. What's the hurry? The journey is so beautiful, why speed through it?'

The girls would giggle. 'Bring your brother along, why does he stay so distant?'

'Why bother him when I am here? He has his fantasies to give him company. Must be dreaming of a horse, I am sure…'

Cold, dry wind ushered them into Rajasthan. Tandhan felt a sense of déjà vu the moment he entered the state, an inexplicable, instant connection to the land. Adjusting his white *pagdi* and wrapping the shawl tighter, he looked at the distant *pagdandi* with wheel marks, telling him about the caravans that had long treaded on the same path to the destination he was headed towards. He then quickly scanned his surroundings for any suspicious person or activity. Often, on paths like these, dacoits ambushed travellers and robbed them. Even the Mughals were known to kidnap youth and young women to make them their slaves or impregnate them to increase their population.

Tandhan's eyes met Ranaji's who was leading the group, mounted on his horse. He waved to Tandhan and asked him to come forward. He jumped down from the horse and let Tandhan ride it instead. He mounted the horse in one clean leap and looked mischievously at Ranaji, communicating his question in silence. Ranaji smiled and nodded.

Euphoric, Tandhan patted the horse's back and rode at a speed that could challenge even a cheetah. In no time, he had left the caravan behind. In front of him, a little further away, he could see colourful tents and barricades. Tandhan stopped to look behind for the group but they were nowhere in sight. Thirsty and hungry, he decided to wait for them at the fair. He tied the horse at the stable allocated for visitors and paid a few coins to the attendant. He then dusted his clothes, adjusted his pagdi and the sword hanging from the waistband tied over his *kurta*, and made his way to the first shop in sight selling food—*jalebi* and *mirchi pakora*.

Gulping down a glass of Persian rose *sherbet*, he ordered a plate of each. As he sipped on the second glass of the red-coloured *sharbat*, he watched the *akhara* on his left where a hefty boy was reducing a much smaller opponent to dust. The arrogance and aggression in his manner was evident. After defeating the small boy, he immediately pounced on the next one even before the referee could signal the start of the duel.

The *akhara* was full of wrestlers of similar bulky build who appeared more like goons, bullying others. Although the *jalebi* was juicy, Tandhan was far too distracted by the duel in the *akhara* to truly savour its taste. He was agitated by the actions and behaviour of the wrestler who by now had lifted a *lathi* to fight against his weaponless opponent whose skills were overpowering his. Fearing his wrath, no one protested from the crowd and with a blow, he fractured the opponent's arm. Seeing this, Tandhan got up and walked towards the *akhara*, his plate of food barely touched.

'What you just did is cheating. Be a man and fight fair', he shouted.

His opponent lay on the ground, writhing in pain.

The boy looked at Tandhan, his face contorted in unmistakable disdain. No one had ever raised a voice against him. He walked to the periphery of the *akhara* where Tandhan stood. Placing both his hands on the bamboo barricade, he bent low and looked straight into Tandhan's eyes. Tandhan stepped forward, his gaze steady.

'If you know the rules so well, you must surely know how to fight too. Let's see how much of a man you are.'

Tandhan considered for a moment. His caravan had not yet arrived and he was only carrying a sword. He certainly had no *lathi*. As if reading his thoughts, the wrestler threw a *lathi* in his direction.

'Don't worry, I will play by the rules this time. Come,

let's see what you've got.'

By now, Tandhan was burning with fury. The wrestler's arrogance was unbearable. He slipped out of his *kurta*, tightened his *dhoti* and removed his *pagdi*. After placing it on a nearby bench along with his sword, he stepped inside.

'Har Har Mahadev!'

Tandhan bent down and paid his reverence to the moist soil of the *akhara*, then smeared some on his bare, sculpted body. A hush fell over the crowd. Who was this brave, handsome boy who had dared to take on the most feared bully? The wrestler with the broken arm looked at Tandhan in awe.

'Be careful, *bhaiya*, he is an unethical monster', he said.

Without warning, the wrestler charged towards Tandhan. Having anticipated the move, Tandhan slipped under his arm and placed a hard blow from behind. The wrestler immediately fell to the ground, his face smeared with mud. Growling in fury, he got up and leapt at Tandhan yet again but he was too slow. Moving swiftly, Tandhan wasted his attack yet again. By now the wrestler was restless and furious. He could hear the crowd murmuring. Multiple failed attacks and powerful blows from Tandhan had drained him. He couldn't lose to Tandhan.

He looked at some of his peers and tilted his neck in Tandhan's direction. Getting the signal, five wrestlers with *lathis* jumped inside and circled Tandhan. Facing six wrestlers, some of them far bigger and stronger than him, Tandhan was ready to battle.

All of them attacked at once. Tandhan swung his *lathi* in the air in circles covering the entire *akhara*. The others faltered but kept coming back. Aware that his stamina would run out soon, Tandhan slowed a bit to catch some breath. It was then that one of the wrestlers placed a heavy blow and his *lathi* fell. Just as the main wrestler was about to launch another blow, he let out a scream. His shoulder stuck out at an odd angle and he fell to the ground. Everyone stopped as he winced in pain, screaming for help, and then looked at the perpetrator who had attacked him from behind.

Tandhan's eyes met that of a boy of average height dressed in a white *kurta*, *dhoti*, and *pagdi*. A black cloth covered his entire face. One could see nothing but his eyes. He was now attacking the other wrestlers one by one. Having found an ally, Tandhan picked up his *lathi* and got up. He started attacking the other wrestlers and, one by one, they fell to the ground. Within a couple of minutes, all six wrestlers were lying on the ground. The silence of the crowd turned into loud cheering and applause as the six goons whimpered in pain. Everyone rushed in and lifted Tandhan on their shoulder. Tandhan's eyes followed the other boy as he slipped away from the *akhara*.

He hurriedly dismounted, thanking everyone, and ran behind the boy. It was difficult to catch up with him in the crowd. Standing at a crossroads, he looked in all directions, unable to spot the boy who had helped him. Dejected, he started walking back to collect his belongings. Just then, at a tent a little further away, he saw him. He rushed towards the tent.

He was about to step in front of him when he saw the boy drop his *pagdi*. Like a cascade, jet-black hair came hurtling down to his waist. Shocked, Tandhan hid behind the tent and watched as the dhoti came undone to reveal a red *ghaghra*. The *kurta* made way for a green *choli* with an open back to reveal flawless porcelain skin. He looked on, mesmerised. Just then, a shrill call disrupted his reverie. 'Narayani! Narayani!'

'Narayani', he muttered under his breath and slipped inside the empty tent. He wanted to see her, thank her, but for now, he wanted to just let her be.

'Where have you been? *Baba* is looking for you', said Radha. 'He said it's getting late, we have to leave so we can reach Dokwa before dark. Now rush!'

Narayani held Radha's hand. 'No, wait. Let me first buy some red and green bangles from that shop near the *akhara*.'

'You still haven't bought them? You left solely to buy those bangles! What were you doing all this while?'

'It's a long story, I will tell you on the way', she said, pulling her towards the bangles shop.

Tandhan followed the two. Her beauty, strength, and courage had left him awestruck. He kept trying to strike up a conversation with her but words wouldn't escape him.

The girls finally reached the shop and Narayani started choosing bangles for herself.

'Can I pay for these bangles as a token of thanks for saving my life?' He said.

Narayani looked at him in shock. *How did he find her?* Her shock soon made way for awe as she looked at his handsome face. His eyes and voice carried in them an ocean of truth. In silence, they looked at each other, and with suspicion, Radha looked at them both.

'May I, Narayani?' Tandhan asked.

'Huh?' Narayani looked at him, dumbfounded. His lips moved but she heard nothing.

Radha nudged Narayani.

'Narayani, please allow me to pay for these.'

How did he know her name? Never had her name sounded sweeter. She continued to look at him, her cheeks turning redder by the minute, her heart beating so loud that she feared he would hear it. Radha pulled Narayani to the side. 'Who is he? And how does he know you?'

Abhimanyu.

Tandhan smiled and stepped forward. 'I am Tandhan, son of Diwan Jaliram Bansal, the Diwan of Hisar. Now, can I pay for the bangles? You saved my life…as a token of my gratitude, please let me buy them for you.'

Narayani nodded, her movement stiff as a robot. The shopkeeper handed over the bangles wrapped in a paper parcel. Tandhan made the payment.

'Let's go! *Baba* is going to leave us here for sure', said Radha, pulling Narayani by her arm.

Tandhan and Narayani's eyes did not waver off each other until the distance between them grew so far apart that they dissolved into the darkness.

'Where have you two been?' said Ganga. 'Did you get the bangles that you wanted?'

Jolting out of her trance, Narayani looked at Radha dazed. Both nodded and said nothing of the incident involving Tandhan. Seated in the cart, Tandhan's act of bravery kept playing before Narayani's eyes. His courage and righteousness in the *akhara* and his humility were spellbinding. He was different, unlike any other boy she had ever met.

She was describing to Radha the fight in the *akhara*, Tandhan's every move to attack and defend, his valour and courage, the cowardice of the other wrestlers and their eventual defeat. On and on she went narrating, oblivious to the fact that Radha had long fallen asleep. She would keep touching her bangles and shaking her arms to see them catch the light and whisper, 'Abhimanyu! No, Tandhan! Tandhan from Hisar'. With a heart that felt full of an emotion she had never felt before, she finally fell asleep with a smile on her lips, hoping to meet him again in a different place and time.

***

'How many more will go down your stomach?'

Tandhan watched as Kamal picked one more *pakora* from his plate.

'And what took you all so long to reach? I have been walking around here alone for so long…I have never seen a fair like this!'

'We didn't take long', said Kamal eating a *pakora*, 'you flew too fast. And why are your clothes so dirty? Were you really walking around or rolling around to see the fair?'

Tandhan went on to tell his brother about the fight at the *akhara* and the faceless boy who had helped him but left Narayani from the narrative. He knew if he told Kamal about Narayani, he would never hear the end of it.

Clenching Tandhan's shoulder from behind, Ranaji asked with concern, 'Are you alright? You have done me proud, yet again…and where is that brave little boy who came to your rescue? We should all thank him together for helping you'.

'I am fine. The boy disappeared immediately after the fight.'

Narayani's skill as a wrestler and her enchanting beauty, like that of an angel, had consumed him. Just the thought of her would make him break into an involuntary smile as they went about the fair. The brothers cheered together at the camel race, gorged on different delicacies, and bought rare spices from Arab traders. Tandhan looked at many horses and enquired about their breeds but none suited his taste.

'We must have seen fifty horses by now and you still don't find any worthy of your ownership? *Bhaiya*, you are impossible', said Kamal.

Tandhan then went to the same bangle shop where he had met Narayani. There, he ran his hands over the bangles that Narayani had touched.

'Now you want to wear bangles? There must have been something wrong with the food, your mind seems to have been affected', said Kamal.

Tandhan tapped on Kamal's head. 'Let's buy these for *maa*', he said.

Tandhan chose the same bangles that Narayani had bought. Kamal looked at his brother, amused. His behaviour seemed unusual. The brothers next bought a carpet from a Persian store for Jaliram to use while offering prayers. After spending several hours shopping and exploring the fair, they lay down to sleep in the tents rented by their fellow villagers.

Head resting on palms turned upwards and eyes on the lantern hanging from the entrance of the tent, Tandhan's thoughts wandered, yet again, to now familiar streets—Narayani, her beauty, and strength. Her powerful, clean blows with the *lathi* had floored wrestlers twice her size, making them taste the dust. Her focus and ability to intercept and react to the movement of enemies she had her back to was remarkable. Above all, her ability to transform from a warrior to an angelic beauty was nothing short of magical. He remembered in vivid detail the way her thick, black hair had cascaded down her waist, the delicate curls that kissed her cheeks, her eyes lined with kohl that bore the depths of her soul and her smile that soothed the heart. 'Now I know that *apsaras* tread the earth as well', he thought to himself and blushed.

She was exactly what he dreamt of, a woman as strong as she was delicate—a complete woman. His heart ached to reach out to her, longed for another meeting and he recalled Radha's words. *We have to reach Dokwa before sunset.* He sighed and turned to his side. He knew he would not see her again. Suddenly, he heard loud sounds of *lathis* and angry voices. He got up with a start; as did Kamal and Ranaji. They leapt off the charpoy and went outside.

Half a dozen men were throwing the belongings of a seller to the ground. One of them held the seller by his collar.

'You fool! Don't you know you have to pay a tax to us as well for putting up this stall?'

The villager joined his hands. 'What tax are you talking about? I have already paid my share. No other tax is levied here', he said with his hands joined, his entire being trembling in fear.

Ranaji, Tandhan, and Kamal positioned themselves behind the seller, their weapons drawn. Letting go of the seller's collar, the man turned to Ranaji. 'Give us our share of grains and livestock and we will do no damage.'

By now, other sellers and travellers who had been bullied by the group stood behind Tandhan and looked straight into the goon's eyes.

'No other tax or demand that is illegal will be

entertained by us. As for the damage done by all of you, every spilt grain will be repaid by your blood.'

Seeing the villagers in such large numbers, the group withdrew and walked away. Tandhan grabbed one of them and pulled him back.

'Put that bag of grain back on the heap.'

The altercation ended on a sweet note for the villagers and it was back to merriment for the two brothers and the rest of the group. Another day of shopping, exploration, and gluttony followed. On their last day, Tandhan traced his steps back to all those places where he had spent precious few moments with Narayani—the *akhara*, the tent, and the bangle shop. He was taking back beautiful memories and the image of the girl he would want to hold hands with and have as his life partner.

'*Bhaiya*, you surely have someone beautiful running through your mind who makes you turn pink every now and then', said Kamal.

Tandhan grinned and galloped off.

CHAPTER 13

Durga's Death ⚵

Dokwa

Hurriedly cooling the *chulha*, Ganga rushed towards the room. 'Laado, are you ready or not? Sheila and her family must be waiting, we have to help them with preparations before the *baraat* arrives.'

The moment Ganga stepped into the room, she froze, looking at her daughter in her old wedding dress. It fit her as though it had been made for her. With her head covered, a golden *barolo* on the forehead, a nose ring covering her right cheek, and a big red dot on her forehead, she looked like a bride herself.

'See *maa*, your dress fits me so well…as if it was stitched for me. How do I look? It's my friend's wedding and I wanted to look the best. What do you think?'

Gurshamal entered the room and froze too. Laado dressed in her mother's wedding dress was nothing short of a spectacle.

'Will someone please tell me how I look? Why are

you two staring and not speaking?' Narayani said.

Ganga stepped forward. Taking some *kajal* from her eyes, she put a *tikka* behind Narayani's ear. 'My *beti* looks grown up and as beautiful as her mother.'

Together, the family went to attend the wedding. Unlike their daughter who was bubbling with enthusiasm, Gurshamal and Ganga appeared to have grown quiet. Throughout the ceremony, the two kept looking at Narayani, weaving dreams for their daughter's future, overwhelmed that it was time they started preparing for her inevitable farewell. They saw how beautiful she looked, how hospitable and warm she was in her conduct, and how the whole village ran their hands on her head praising and blessing her.

'Dear, I think it's time we begin finding a match for Laado', she said.

Gurshamal got up in a haste to refill his plate with *puris*. 'You have lost your mind', he said. 'She is too young for marriage. And I don't think I am getting her married ever.'

Ganga's eyes filled with tears on hearing Gurshamal's words. He sounded so weak and helpless.

'*Maa*, come quickly! The *baraat* is almost here. It is so big with so many people! Everyone is dressed so well and look at all the gifts they have brought for Sheila. Come *maa*, let's dance with the procession.'

Lila grabbed Narayani by the arm. 'Girls do not dance in public. Stay here.'

Narayani frowned. After the many rituals and *pheras*,

Sheila dipped her palms in vermillion waters and left red handprints on the walls of her house signifying the memories that she was leaving behind. She then voluntarily chose to place her red-coloured hands, considered auspicious, on Narayani's head to bless her with a marriage soon. Narayani in turn hugged her with gratitude and love. From a *jhola*, she took out a palm-sized doll that she had made of clay, dressed in a beautiful red dress, and handed it to Sheila.

'Sheila, take this doll as me, your friend. Whenever you feel lonely and want to talk to someone, talk to her and tell her everything. Do not keep things in your heart, my friend, for that is how they turn toxic. We will miss you, Sheila.'

The friends hugged again, this time much longer than before, and Sheila finally sat in the *palki* to leave for a new home.

Tired after an entire day's celebration, Narayani slept immediately upon reaching home, her face smeared with dried tears, clutching tight a doll. Ganga and Gurshamal looked at their daughter for long, deep in thought. Once they lay down in bed, Gurshamal placed his head on Ganga's lap and wept like a child.

'Ganga, I know…I can see Narayani is grown up and has reached an age where we should start finding a match for her. But even the thought of sending my laado away is so painful. I feel so insecure…how will the boy and his family treat my princess? I don't know what will I do without her around…I think I will break, Ganga, I don't have the courage to get my daughter married. Let's keep her with us forever.'

'I can understand your pain, for mine is the same. But we have to do our duty and do what is best for her. And why worry about the future, she is a very good child… Lord Narayan will ensure she has a happy married life. Let's just put our faith in the almighty and perform our duties', Ganga said, stroking his hair.

The subject of Narayani's wedding did not come up again in the next few days. Ganga was aware that Gurshamal was intentionally avoiding it. He did not want to get Narayani married. Day by day, Ganga was growing livid. One evening, Ganga's vessels and utensils were making a lot more noise than usual as she cooked dinner. She skipped her usual evening *sadhana* with Gurshamal and her face perpetually bore her feeling of anger. While cleaning the kitchen after dinner, she even forgot to keep the burning coal for the fire and poured water on the *chulha*.

'Narayani, go to Lila *tai*'s house and bring some fire.'

Narayani knew by her mother's tone that she was furious and it was best to leave her alone until she calmed down. While she was away to fetch the fire, Gurshamal sat his wife down and asked her the reason behind her behaviour.

'I want you to take laado's *kundali* (horoscope chart) to the local Brahmin and ask him to find a match for her. Do you even realise that in spite of her being so beautiful and popular, no one has ever proposed marriage? Do you realise her abilities that surpass most boys can become a challenge for her to get married? You are blinded by your love for her.'

'Ganga, we all come down to the earth in pairs… even if no one has proposed yet, someone out there who was made just for her is waiting. When the time comes, he will appear.'

Ganga was about to reply when Narayani came running into the house.

'*Maa! Baba!* Radha is getting married. Lila *tai* just told me that they have arranged her marriage to a boy from the next village. All my friends are getting married and leaving, now I will be left alone, no one to play with.'

'See!' Ganga looked at Gurshamal, fire spewing from her eyes. Without uttering another word, she went to sleep. Gurshamal stayed up long after midnight, thinking about how and where to find a boy who could match the calibre of his daughter. She was different and special and deserved a similar match. The next morning, as Gurshamal picked up his *jhola* to leave, Ganga handed him Narayani's *kundali*.

'Go and ask Panditji when the right time is and who the right boy is.'

With a heavy heart, Gurshamal nodded and left, staring at the rolled-up paper in his hand. He started walking to the Brahmin's house, his mind heavy with thoughts. *I have to be strong. And why should I worry, this paper has already been inked with Narayani's fate by the stars. As the wise seer had said, she is destiny's child, the chosen one. Her fate holds nothing but the best.*

Standing in front of the wooden blue door, Gurshamal took a deep breath. He then knocked on it with the iron handle. A lady with her head covered greeted and escorted him in. Gurshamal entered with his back hunched to avoid bumping his head on the small frame. While he waited for the astrologer to finish his daily puja, Gurshamal wondered yet again. Was it really the right time to find a match for his daughter? He then reminded himself that every ten-year-old girl in the village was already married and Narayani was twelve.

Guruji finally emerged.

'You have come at an auspicious time, Gurshamal *ji*...right after the puja is when my mind is clearest to study the planets and stars and follow my intuition. Tell me, how can I help you?'

Gurshamal touched his feet and offered a packet of fruits and sweets. 'Guruji, I have brought my Narayani's *kundali* with me...I want you to tell me about her marriage *dasha*.'

Gurshamal observed with anxiety as Guruji studied the *kundali*. Bowing down before Mata Saraswati, Guruji spoke, 'You need not worry at all about Narayani. Her stars need no study, her destiny is so well inscribed that people and circumstances will autonomously be drawn to her to fulfil it. Her marriage *dasha* has already begun and there is a wedding soon. You should definitely go ahead.'

Thanking him with relief, Gurshamal placed the *kundali* aside. 'But Guruji, I do not see any boy or family worthy of my daughter here in this village. She deserves someone of equal qualities.'

Guruji laughed. 'Now you are talking like a father, plagued with excessive love for your only child, that too, a daughter. If you feel there isn't a suitable match here, I am leaving for a pilgrimage towards the north tomorrow. On my way, when I meet other fellow astrologers, I shall discuss with them and ask them to find the best match for her.'

Happy with the suggestion and grateful that Ganga would now spare him of her wrath, he gave the *kundali* to Guruji and left with a lighter mind.

Later that night, Narayani woke up from deep sleep with a jolt. 'Thank god it was just a dream', she said in relief, wiping pearls of perspiration off her forehead. It was almost dawn. Her parents were fast asleep. Unable to fall back to sleep, she strolled out, seeking comfort after her disturbing dream.

Juggli was up, and on seeing Narayani, started moving around so that her anklet jingled. Narayani picked up a fresh bunch of grass and fed her while running her hand across Juggli's back.

'You know, Juggli, I had a weird dream…I saw Radha getting married and walking away with her groom, holding his hand and leaving behind the whole family. His face was covered with a *shera* (floral veil). On reaching home, he removed the *shera* to reveal his face…he was like a demon, dark and wrinkled with stained teeth and a hunched back. And I saw that he bit Radha on her neck and she fainted. Thank god, it was just a dream.'

The idea of marrying a stranger disturbed Narayani immensely. While she was narrating the incident to Juggli, dawn waited minutes away to break free. Just then, she heard footsteps outside their house. It seemed unusual that someone in the village would wake up so early. She looked towards the room in which her parents lay asleep, then giving in to her curiosity Narayani walked with measured steps to see the person strolling outside at such an odd hour. Holding a lantern in one hand, she slowly opened the gate and put one leg out. As she bent forward to look, she saw the back of a familiar-looking girl, her hair messed up, clothes tattered and a peculiar walk as though she was not a human but a statue made of stone.

Narayani wondered who it could be. She lifted the lantern and moved a little further for a better view. She noticed that the girl's right elbow was bleeding profusely onto her forearm and dripping down her fingers. Then she saw a black band on the wrist. 'Durga?' She whispered in horror and confusion.

The girl kept walking like a ghost without responding to Narayani or reacting to her injury. Still in doubt, Narayani kept watching the figure and took a few more steps ahead. Dawn broke. The figure kept walking. Narayani kept following her, not knowing what to do or expect. A little further away sat a well. The figure and Narayani both kept walking towards it. Before she knew what was happening, the figure reached the well and jumped right in. Narayani let out a scream and collapsed.

When she returned to consciousness, she leapt up,

screaming, 'Durga, stop! Stop!'

Ganga immediately reached out to her. 'Laado, calm down. Here, drink some water.'

Ignoring her mother, Narayani looked around perplexed. It was already noon, she could tell by the harsh light and lack of shadows. She was certainly not dreaming. She clutched her mother's hand. '*Maa*, Durga...I saw her jump. Did she? Why? What happened? Why did she do it? She jumped...' Narayani fell unconscious yet again. It was late evening when she gained consciousness, burning with fever.

Vaidji got up and handed over two medicines wrapped in a paper parcel. 'Let her rest. Mix this one pouch in milk and make her drink it. I will come again tomorrow. Repeat the wet towel treatment to bring down the fever. She is in shock, keep her company.'

Gurshamal's hand burnt as he touched her forehead. Ganga brought the milk mixed with medicine as *vaidji* had instructed, but Narayani refused it. Only tears rolled down her shocked eyes that could not erase the image of Durga jumping into the well.

'Drink, Laado. It will cure you, *bitiya*', said Gurshamal.

'Why did she do it, *baba*? What happened that she took this extreme step? She was always a happy girl. I cannot even—'

Gurshamal handed over the glass to her. 'Drink this and I will tell you what happened.'

Narayani took a sip.

'Yesterday morning', said Gurshamal, 'when Durga was returning with a pot of water, she was attacked and kidnapped by dacoits. She fought them and escaped in the night and reached the village.'

'Then why did she kill herself when she managed to return safely?'

Gurshamal heaved a sigh. Turning his back towards Narayani and looking at the Lord's image, he spoke, 'All the doors of the houses were closed so she had no choice but to open the door of heaven'.

'Narayani,' Ganga intervened, 'when a girl has been away from her home in the dark, she never finds the light of life again. It is sad but it is the truth, my child.'

Narayani sobbed, unable to understand her mother's words, and fell asleep at some point. For days she remained bedridden and gradually understood what had happened. Almost overnight, Narayani grew several years older.

CHAPTER 14

Matchmaking †

Hisar

'Jai Annapurna!' Sprinkling water in a circle around the thali, the Brahmin astrologer consumed his meal in delight.

'Your hands cook like Annapurna, *beti*. You have satiated both my stomach and soul. May God bless you with another Annapurna in your kitchen soon.'

Yamuna bowed down in reverence and lifted the thali. 'Guruji, you have acknowledged my desire and blessed me too, now please show me how to fulfil it.'

Putting his hand inside his saffron bag, he fiddled for a while and removed a beaded necklace. 'Sit in the kitchen and recite Annapurna's name 108 times with this *mala* once daily and soon she will bless you with a daughter-in-law who will fill your home with love.'

'*Maa!* You know what, today I was called by the Nawab and he has offered me the post of deputy manager to look after financial matters along with assistant *subedar* under Ranaji, and he…'

Tandhan stopped talking as he saw the seated Brahmin. He touched his feet then took his thali from his mother's hands and put it inside. Impressed by Tandhan's manners and accomplishment, the Brahmin, who was about to leave, stood thoughtfully for a while. He reached into his bag and pulled out a rolled sheet of paper and handed it to Yamuna.

'It seems Devi Annapurna has already blessed you. This is the *kundali* of a remarkable girl who seems to be the perfect match for your remarkable son. Take it and consult it with your family astrologer. I shall be passing by here again after five days, till then ask Jaliramji to look into the proposal and revert to me on my return. I shall meet him at the shop and share the details before I leave.'

Yamuna's face lit up. She touched his feet and took the *kundali* from him. At dinner, Jaliram praised Tandhan. 'Beta, you have brought us immense pride. Now, since you have been bestowed with this responsibility, perform it with utmost dedication and sincerity.'

'Yes, baba! You and Ranaji are my idols and I will certainly follow in your footsteps.'

'My dreams are also about to become a reality', interrupted Yamuna with a smile on her face. 'The Brahmin has given me a *kundali* he believes will be the right match for our Tandhan. Tomorrow I shall go to Guruji and do the matchmaking.'

'Thank you for reminding me! The Brahmin met

me and told me about the father of the girl, a popular chilli trader who is also a good Samaritan—Gurshamal from Dokwa. I have heard a lot about the man and his family; they are good people. Go to Guruji tomorrow in the morning itself.'

As Tandhan heard the name Dokwa, his heart skipped a beat and the image of Narayani floated before his eyes.

'Bhaiya is already blushing. The groom is ready', Kamal said and laughed.

The next day, Yamuna went to Guruji early in the morning.

'It seems that the stars have been placed keeping these two in mind. I have never seen any two *kundalis* match so well. It is my firm opinion that you go ahead with the marriage', he told her.

That same day, it was decided that Jaliramji would go to meet the girl and her family.

'I am accompanying your father to Dokwa for the marriage proposal', said Ranaji at the *akhara* the next day. 'If you bribe me well, I will give you detailed information about the girl. And if you like someone secretly, you can tell me that too, and I will help with the matchmaking.'

Tandhan's cheeks turned pink. 'She is a stranger… someone from that area only.'

'Ok! I will find that same girl then for my favourite nephew. Tell me about her…'

'No! It's ok. It was just a passing encounter, I don't know much about her. You and baba find the match.'

Dokwa

'Do not worry. I shall drop the supply at your house on my way. Do not stress your old back.' Gurshamal empathised with the old lady who came to buy chillies for her yearly stock.

'Thank you, *beta*! God bless you!'

Looking up to see Panditji along with two strangers, Gurshamal immediately got up from his seat and paid his reverences.

'Gurshamal ji, the old lady's blessings have become fruitful. Meet Jaliramji and Ranaji from Hisar. They have come to talk about their son's marriage with Narayani. The *gunas* in the *kundali* match as though they have been made for each other since the creation of the universe. He is a renowned man serving as a Diwan at the Nawab's court. And after seeing his son, I can say he is a carbon copy of his father, both in achievements and manners.'

Gurshamal offered them a seat and water. 'Jaliramji, I have heard a lot about the progress of Hisar...and I know that you are the man behind it. I am grateful you have considered Panditji's opinion on this union. Please let me escort you home for refreshment.'

While the other elders engaged in conversation and food, Ranaji looked around for the girl who was being considered for his nephew. As if reading his mind, Gurshamal spoke, 'Narayani is in school now, studying. She will return in a while; you can meet her then.'

Ranaji nodded and hid his discontentment. He was a staunch Rajput and firmly believed that women should be kept in veils and under protection, especially when so many atrocities were being inflicted upon women by barbarians.

'Narayani is an outstanding girl. Unlike others, she is educated and also a perfect homemaker. Her many talents have earned her a popularity that surpasses all the boys and girls in this village. She is truly a Devi's avatar', Panditji intervened, reading Ranaji's thoughts yet again.

'Panditji is being generous', said Gurshamal.

'Why not let girls be girls?' Ranaji said.

'I am happy to know, Gurshamal ji, that you have raised your daughter so well', said Jaliramji before Gurshamal could answer. 'We shall take your leave now to reach Hisar on time. Please visit us soon to meet Tandhan and our family. By then, I will also consult with my wife Yamuna regarding the proposal.'

'After meeting you, my worries have lessened. If Tandhan is your replica, then he is surely the groom for my daughter. I shall visit soon with Ganga.'

'Gurshamal ji, you surely like to involve women everywhere', said Ranaji.

Jaliram smiled and took Gurshamal's leave.

Once they were out of the house and away from audible reach, Ranaji broke his silence.

'How can you consider a girl who is so outgoing and independent for Tandhan? You think she will be an obedient wife and daughter-in-law who abides by all the rules?'

'Humph!' Jaliram was preoccupied with other

thoughts and decided not to pay too much heed to Ranaji's cynicism.

Once Jaliram reached home, tired after the long journey, he said his prayers and immediately went to bed.

Unable to hold back his curiosity, Tandhan left, announcing that he was going out for some work.

'What work do you have at this hour?' Yamuna asked.

Before Tandhan could reply, Kamal Ram spoke, half-asleep in bed, 'He has work with Ranaji. He wants to know what happened'.

In no time, Tandhan reached Ranaji's house.

'Come! I was expecting you. I know the night is too long for all your questions to wait.'

Seating Tandhan, he looked into his eyes and said, 'I could not find the girl of your dreams. The one we went to see was away at school and as per her father and Panditji's description, she seems to be a disobedient, untamed girl who breaks all rules of the village. But Panditji says she is a special girl, an avatar of a Devi; your father already likes her. I am not in favour of this union. What kind of a girl behaves like a boy? And why would anyone approve of such a girl?'

'Is her name Narayani?' Tandhan asked, almost certain it was her.

Ranaji nodded. 'Yes. Why?'

Tandhan hugged him in euphoria. 'She is the girl of my dreams, Ranaji. She is the one I met at Pushkar. She is the one I want to marry. Oh Ranaji, I am so happy!'

Tandhan told him everything that had happened

inside the *akhara* at the fair. He told him of how he had been thinking about her day and night.

Ranaji flung his hands in the air. 'What can I say when you have already made a choice? May Goddess Bhavani bless you!'

Back from school, Narayani had barely removed her *jhola* when Ganga stuffed a *laddoo* in her mouth.

'Laado, there's good news. The Diwan of Hisar was here. He wants you to become his daughter-in-law. They are very reputed people, and Panditji says their son is a gem of a boy. Your baba and I will go and meet the family soon. My Laado is going to be a bride.'

When she heard Hisar and Diwan, Narayani was reminded of Pushkar. While still gorging on the *laddoo*, she inquired, 'Even I will come along, right?'

Ganga looked at Narayani in a sombre way. 'Laado, girls don't meet their grooms before marriage.'

For the rest of the day, Narayani appeared distant and withdrawn. Gurshamal assumed it was because Narayani was feeling shy. But later during the day, she proved him wrong.

'Baba, I know you love me the most. And I know you have this vast life experience that helps you tell wrong from right. But baba, marrying an unknown person in an unknown place is scary and unacceptable. Can't I at least meet and see the boy once? My entire life depends on this one decision…'

'Now you are being too demanding and using your head too much, Laado! Ganga, please explain to her!'

Narayani lowered her head and walked away. Ganga and Gurshamal shared a long thoughtful silence, helplessness written all over their faces. Like a diligent daughter, Narayani cooked the meal meant to be packed for the long journey the next day. Following her mother's instructions, she also packed two packets of *laddoo* and *sooji ka seera*.

Just as dawn broke, Ganga and Gurshamal, along with Panditji, sat in the cart to leave for Hisar. Narayani watched with a forced smile on her lips. The cart started moving and Narayani remained still, letting the distance between them grow. The cart had barely crossed three houses when Ganga asked the rider to stop.

'Narayani, come with us!'

Hearing Ganga's words, Gurshamal, seated next to the rider, turned around and looked at her with a questioning glance.

'Let her come. It is natural for a girl to feel curious and apprehensive in this situation.'

Gurshamal, although unsure, nodded his head.

'It's okay', said Panditji, 'she will not join us. We can ask her to wait at the temple opposite their house. I know the Brahmin there.'

Narayani hopped into the cart, delighted more than she was willing to show.

As the cart stopped outside Jaliram's house, Kamal Ram, who was tending to the heap of wood for the fire, looked up. Recognising Panditji, he rushed inside to call his mother. Ganga and Gurshamal tidied their clothes in a hurry and carried with them the packet of sweets they had brought along. Her *odhani* over her head, Yamuna came to greet them with a warm smile and ushered them into the house. Seating them on the charpoy in the covered courtyard adjacent to the big, open courtyard, Yamuna asked Kamal to inform his father about their arrival and then bring Tandhan home.

Ganga was in awe of the house. She had never seen one so big. The main house was built with bricks and coloured beautifully, unlike the thatched ones in their village. In the shed were three cows and a horse. As the men sat down, Ganga joined Yamuna to assist her. Kamal introduced himself and then left to call his father.

'Wait, *beta*! It's an auspicious occasion, please ask Tandhan to visit the temple nearby before coming to meet us', said Panditji.

After a while, Jaliram arrived. 'I hope I didn't keep you waiting for long…how was the journey?'

Gurshamal stood up to meet Jaliram. Ganga and Yamuna emerged from inside, carrying glasses of buttermilk.

Meanwhile, Kamal spotted Tandhan with Ranaji on an inspection round at the infantry.

'Bhaiya! Baba has called you home! The family from Dokwa has arrived for the proposal. Come quick.'

Tandhan's heart skipped a beat and he looked at Ranaji for permission. Ranaji rolled his eyes. 'Go! But I will still advise you to reconsider your decision to marry that girl', he warned.

'Don't worry!'

Tandhan and Kamal broke into a run. While Kamal stopped at the market to buy snacks, Tandhan headed to the temple following his brother's instructions. Quickly removing his slippers, he started running up the stairs, skipping two at a time. He stopped suddenly mid-way, turned to his right, and looked in utter disbelief at the face that had been mesmerising him in his fantasies. The whole world ceased to exist when he saw Narayani reclined under a great, big banyan tree.

Lying on the ground with her eyes closed and head resting on her hands, she was napping in the shade. Tandhan bowed before the deities and then walked towards her, absorbing her beauty with every step. As he moved closer, he saw her baby curls dancing over her face with abandon, her closed eyes lined with kohl, and the little smile on her lips that hinted at a beautiful dream. Hearing his footsteps, she opened her eyes and then closed them again. In a moment, she opened them again with a start and got up.

'Are you real or I am dreaming?' She said.

Tandhan smiled. 'You always have a way of surprising me! I didn't know the Gods were so kind.'

She blushed. 'I had to come…couldn't take a chance. Had to make sure it was you…the one who fits perfectly into my life.'

Tandhan's smile broadened. 'You are truly remarkable! Just the one I have always searched for. Now, if you will allow me to go and announce my wish for this union…'

Heart bursting with joy, Narayani lowered her eyes and nodded.

Tandhan walked to his house with quick steps, his soul ready to fly out of him and somersault. From the moment Gurshamal saw Tandhan, he knew this was the boy he would get his daughter married to. His warm and gentle manner won his heart.

'You took very long to reach here', said Ranaji. 'I am happy you were ruminating over my advice.'

Once Narayani's parents left, Kamal Ram noticed Ranaji talking to Yamuna in the kitchen in private. From their expressions and body language, it was apparent the topic was Tandhan and Narayani's wedding. They didn't seem convinced about the proposal. Later in the evening, Yamuna expressed her doubts before Jaliram. 'How can a girl who has been raised like a boy be a good daughter-in-law?'

'What does the fact that a girl is literate or that she is able to assist her father in work and takes classes for villagers, have anything to do with her not being obedient or a good homemaker?'

Just then, Kamal entered the room with the box of sweets given by Narayani's parents.

'Maa, baba! You have to taste this. I have never eaten anything more delicious! Didn't they say it was prepared by their daughter?'

At first reluctant, when she finally tasted it, Yamuna mellowed.

'See, I told you! She is the perfect match for Tandhan.

And have you not seen your son? How he smiles and blushes every time we mention Narayani! He wants to marry her. So, let's say yes and proceed further with the arrangements.'

The next day, in both Hisar and Dokwa, the news of Tandhan and Narayani's wedding on the ninth phase of the moon in December was announced with much fervour.

Nawab Jhadchand summoned Jaliram and Tandhan to the court.

'I am very happy to hear the news of the marriage, Jaliram! You have my blessing and support for the occasion. Please feel free to demand anything you need. And don't forget to buy the best Arab fabric for the bride and groom!'

Both of them bowed before him and thanked him. Raj Kumar caught up with Tandhan. 'You can take my horse and clothes for your marriage if you wish. They will think you are rich!'

Tandhan shook his head and walked away. Not even the meanest of words could dampen his spirit now.

CHAPTER 15

The Seer's Prediction

Dokwa

'You know, Juggli, he is the most gentle boy I have ever met in my life…and he has the most handsome face too. Baba says there is no one quite like him in the town of Hisar. His strength and intelligence outshine all youth. And the best part, Juggli, is that he wants to marry me just like I want to marry him. Unlike all other families and boys who rejected me because I was too free-willed and independent to be a good homemaker, he sees it as a strength and not a weakness. He is not insecure like the others who feel that my education, martial art skill, and the fact that I assist baba threatens their masculinity. I am sure you will like him as soon as you see him.' Narayani poured her heart out to her childhood companion, Juggli, the calf that had now grown into a cow.

Knock! Knock!

Narayani ran to open the door. In came two men carrying sacks of wheat, which they heaped in the courtyard.

'Shyam *tau*, has baba ordered these?'

He ran his hand over her head. 'No *bitiya*, I brought it on my own. The best wheat from the harvest for your wedding. *Baaratis* should be fed nothing but the best and you should carry along the best grains too.'

'You are truly gracious, Shyam *Bhaaya*!' Gurshamal said, walking into the room. 'But this is too much! I will send the money tomorrow.'

While the adults spoke, Narayani went to fetch water.

'Money? No way! How can you even think I would take money for Narayani's wedding preparations? Gurshamal ji, have you forgotten how your supply of spices has been unending? Now please let us also do something for our dear *bitiya*.'

In the next few weeks, Gurshamal made frequent trips to Hisar, Bhiwani, and Delhi as he shopped for his daughter's wedding. For Narayani, he wanted nothing but the best. From Arab traders, he purchased the finest perfumes and carpets to gift the *baaratis*, and for his dear daughter, he bought the best fabrics money could buy for her trousseau. The goldsmith had a hard time catering to Gurshamal, who was very particular not only about the purity of the metal but the design as well. While making every purchase, he would imagine them adorning his Laado.

He had already gone over his budget when buying gifts for the *baaratis*. He poured his heart into every detail with little consideration for expenditure. The entire village was gearing up for the upcoming wedding. People decked up the exteriors of their homes with fresh paint to make a good impression on the *baarat* that was going to arrive from a different town, that too from an affluent and popular family. Various traders and sellers thronged Gurshamal's shop, offering whatever best they had, knowing well that he was rich as well as generous when it came to his daughter.

'Gurshamal ji, I have brought the rarest of horses for you, one which has arrived from lands far, far away; a breed known for its exemplary strength and speed. Though I can trade it for a good price in Delhi, I felt it would be a one-of-a-kind gift for your son-in-law. Have a look if you wish', said the Arab horse trader who had delivered Narayani's horse.

It was a very handsome horse, a stunning light brown colour that shone like gold in the daylight. It stood very tall too and looked like it belonged to a king. The Arab horse trader had rightly described him—rarest of rare. Gurshamal immediately purchased it for an exorbitant price. He imagined Tandhan seated on it and smiled at the image.

Back at their house, the space was getting congested with the heaps of supplies being stocked for the wedding. Every day, women were at their house cleaning grains, grinding spices, and storing them in fresh, new jars. Big containers were slowly filling with the kitchen necessities that Narayani would carry with her. The entire village was working together to ensure that everything came together perfectly for the day of Narayani's wedding.

Cooling the *chulha* and lowering the flames of all the

lanterns, Ganga wiped her hands on her *odhani* and sat down, exhausted, next to Gurshamal. They both looked at Narayani's face as she slept in peace. Their whole world revolved around her.

'Have all the preparations been made or is anything pending? Please make sure nothing is missed. I have arranged the stay for the whole *baarat* a few miles away with all the comfort and security they might need. And let us check the box as well. Let's do it now, it's safe at this hour.'

Ganga took a lantern and headed to Amba's thatch. There, she pushed the big vessel of water kept for Amba. Gurshamal looked around to make sure no one was watching and slid the heavy block of stone to reveal a hole in the ground containing a big steel box. Keeping it as quiet as possible, the two carried it to their room. Wiping perspiration off his forehead, Gurshamal lifted the lid. It contained hundreds of silver and gold coins.

'I think this much will suffice for Laado's wedding… to gift to the family?'

Ganga nodded. 'Are you sure you want to give away your life savings? Don't you think we should keep some?'

'She is a piece of my heart! What will we do with all this money? We have a flourishing business that supplies us with enough to lead a comfortable life. Why keep any?'

Ganga nodded. After all, Narayani was their only child.

***

Sita, Radha, Sheila, and Narayani were playing with their dolls near the pond. They had built a *mandap* with twigs and grass and decorated it with flowers and accessories. Radha's girl doll was getting married to Sheila's boy doll. Together they sang songs and made them move in circles. In the end, Radha's doll left with Sheila's.

'But I have created it with my hands, how can I just give her away like that? I don't want to play this game. I won't give her away. Give me back my doll!' Radha cried.

The other friends consoled her. 'Radha, this is a tradition. She has to go and build her home. You can't back off now. And don't worry, Sheila will keep her well. She will give her better dresses than you do.'

Ganga and Lila were washing clothes nearby, listening to the girls' conversation.

'Isn't this the irony of our lives too? Our little dolls whom we raised with so much love will depart immediately after the *pheras* to embrace a home unknown to them. Isn't society harsh to have made such traditions? Even I don't wish to play this game.'

Both the mothers soothed each other and prayed that their dolls find a home that would keep them happy and safe.

***

'*Alak Niranjan*! Gurshamal, where are you? It has been years since I last came here. The whole village was rejoicing your daughter's birth then and now it is decked up for her marriage. I am happy to see that your affluence and popularity have grown over the years. I heard of the union of the two well-known families. Won't you give this Brahmin something to eat?' It was the seer who had visited them many years ago.

Gurshamal escorted the Brahmin with reverence. Ganga appeared with a *lota* of water and a plate to wash his feet.

'Call your daughter, let me bless her and read her palms to study her fate.'

Gurshamal immediately called for Narayani.

'She still bears the *tej* of a Devi, someone chosen by destiny for something bigger. *Bitiya*, show me your left hand, let me see what your future holds.'

Narayani opened her palm.

'But Baba, how can these lines speak of my future? They are simple lines on the palm.'

'Just like no two people share similar fates, no two people ever carry the same lines. God draws them individually, just as he makes everyone unique in their own way. With practice and intuition, one can read these and predict the future', he explained. As he spoke, his face grew tense. He removed a piece of broken glass from his bag and looked more closely through it. He kept studying her palm for a long time.

'Are my lines difficult to read, Baba?' She asked, curious.

'What's the matter, Baba, you look tense. Is everything

ok?' Gurshamal asked.

The Brahmin did not answer and took Narayani's right hand, believed to be the hand of the husband. After studying it for a while, he got up, enraged.

'All the astrologers you consulted are fools! How have they matched the stars for this marriage? It is clearly visible in her palm that her husband has a very short life. If she marries him, she will be a widow in a year's time.'

The *thaal* filled with sweets, fruits, clothes, and money, which Ganga had carried to offer the Brahmin, fell to the ground with a loud thud as she fell unconscious. Narayani rushed to attend to her, but Gurshamal did not react, frozen stiff by the prediction. Regaining consciousness, Ganga rushed to the seer and fell to his feet.

'Baba, please give us a solution. How can we change Narayani's fate?'

'The future cannot be altered, it can either be accepted or destroyed. I leave the decision to you. I can only predict what's coming, it's for you to take relevant action.'

The seer left. Narayani escorted her weak mother to her room. Gurshamal had no reaction to the seer's abrupt departure. His face bore a singular expression—shock.

'That was just a prediction, he could be wrong, in fact, he is…they all are. My future is not trapped in the lines of my palms but in the choices I make and the actions I perform. You both should not be taking his words seriously', said Narayani.

Ganga walked to Gurshamal. 'What are you thinking?

Leave immediately for Hisar and call off the wedding. There is no need for any further discussion here.'

'NOOOOOOO!' Narayani screamed. 'What is wrong with you, maa? You are calling off my marriage just because of what one seer told you. Please calm down and think objectively. Tandhan is a healthy boy, their family is well-to-do, what can possibly go wrong with him? Please don't overthink, maa.'

In silence, Ganga grabbed Narayani by the arm, pushed her into a room and shut it close. 'Stay here without any further display of your wisdom and analysis. You haven't grown big enough to understand these things!'

While Ganga paced the room agitated, Gurshamal sat before the image of Lord Narayan to regain his calm and clarity. Even before the night could descend, the house sat cloaked in darkness, a stark contrast to only a few hours before when it had bustled with joy and excitement. No one lit the lanterns, no one spoke a word.

Lila knocked on the door. When no one answered, she pushed the door open slowly and stepped in. 'Is everything alright? Why is the house dark?'

Seeing Ganga slumped near the pillar sobbing and Gurshamal seated, stiff as a rock, she knew the answer to her first question. Something was not quite right. She attended to Ganga and soothed her. In horror, she heard Ganga relive the moment the seer had shared his prediction with them.

'Even after knowing all this, her father is thinking... not leaving to call off the marriage. Lord Vishnu only knows what has gotten into his head. And that girl is impossible!' Ganga said, her nostrils flaring.

'He is right, Ganga! It is not a joke to call off an engagement. Who will ever approve of Narayani if her wedding is called off for no apparent reason? Her future will be tarnished forever', said Lila. 'Think about it with a calm mind. Where is Narayani?'

The moment Lila received an answer, she stood and unlocked the door. Narayani ran to her father and hugged him tight. 'Baba, please don't do this. Don't believe the seer's words. Look! Can you read anything in my palm that says Tandhan will die soon? Please baba! Don't you remember your own words when you told me not to try and bring the future into the present? That doing so will distort the now? Have you forgotten your own lessons?'

'I am a father, Laado! I love you too much to allow anything bad to happen to you', said Gurshamal, breaking his silence.

Ganga walked up to her husband. 'Don't listen to her or anyone else. I don't care what anyone says. She will remain in this house all her life but I will not be able to see her in white attire, her life drained of all colours and flavours. I'd rather keep her with me than see her die every day.'

Narayani went running into her room and collapsed onto her bed, sobbing, feeling alone and helpless. The next morning, as Gurshamal packed to leave for Hisar, Narayani got up, washed her face, tied her hair, fed Juggli, and then walked straight to Lord Narayan's image. Taking it down, she walked towards Gurshamal and stood in front of him looking right into his eyes. Watching her do this, Ganga left the *chulha* and stood beside Gurshamal.

'In the presence of the Lord', she said, holding the image in her hands, 'I announce, I have taken Tandhan as my groom and promised him my whole heart. I will walk beside him not just for this life but for all my other lives too. Like Mata Sita, I will keep my promise irrespective of the consequence. Like Draupadi, I will fight all customs and traditions if needed. Do not misinterpret my conviction for disobedience. I cannot see my life without him…and it doesn't matter even if it lasts for a day. I am sorry, Maa! I am sorry, Baba! Please try to understand me. Either I marry Tandhan or no one.'

Before either parent could react, there was a knock on the door. It was Masterji. He had learnt of the seer's prediction and the family's reaction to it.

'I understand your pain and anxiety, Gurshamalji', he said, 'but you are breaking the engagement and her heart just because of a seer's prediction! You are a reasonable man, Gurshamalji. Have faith in the creator, not in the words of his creation.'

He then turned to Ganga. '*Behan*, I know you are a mother and a mother's heart doesn't understand reason… but it's faith you need to hold on to. Please don't call off the wedding. Trust the lord and resume the preparations.'

Reminded of their faith in the lord, the couple threw themselves in front of the lord's image, sobbing.

'Please bless us! Let the seer be wrong, lord.'

CHAPTER 16

The Wedding

Hisar

'No, I want red fabric to be added to the sherwani. I love that colour', said Tandhan to the tailor, who in turn was jittery and tired of showing dozens of patterns and colours, none of which seemed to appeal to Tandhan.

'Yes *Bhaaya*, please get the fabric in the shade he wants. It is his favourite since he has seen my *bhabhi*. Her favourite is his favourite now', teased Kamal Ram.

Annoyed with Tandhan's bickering, Ranaji rolled his eyes. 'Your choices surely aren't manly enough. God knows where I failed to teach you well', he said.

Meanwhile, at home, Tandhan's mother was doing her bit of tailoring too. Yamuna dusted the extra threads off the *shera* once she finished. 'Tandhan, come! Let me see if the *shera* that's going to cover my son's handsome face fits or not.'

Tandhan hugged his mother. 'It will, maa. Who knows me like you do?'

'Don't try to flatter me! Once the *dulhan* arrives, I know you will forget your maa.'

Looking lovingly into Yamuna's eyes, he hugged her yet again. 'Someone who is ingrained into my behaviour as well as thinking, how can she be forgotten?'

Jaliram tapped on Yamuna's shoulder. 'We are blessed to have a smart and loving son.'

The big day arrived. It was the ninth phase of the moon in December. Five bullock carts filled with sweets, clothes, jewellery, and cosmetics for the bride, and camel carts filled with men and women dressed in beautiful attire, followed by horsemen with weapons, were ready to leave for Dokwa for the wedding. The air was full of joy, festivity, banter, and the music of *dhols* and *shehnais*. The *baarat* was a grand show. Nawab Jhadchand himself came to meet Jaliram along with his son Raj Kumar.

'I hope you have not missed out on any preparations, Jaliram? I have brought two elephants for you to take along, one for you and the other for Tandhan's ride. You are no ordinary man. You are a Diwan in Jhadchand's court. Your grandiose shall speak of mine. The people of Dokwa should get a glimpse of our prosperity. That cart there is filled with exquisite perfumes, sweets, *sharbats,* and carpets, all gifts for your *samdhi*. Pamper them well. For the *baraat's* safety, I am sending a dozen more horsemen. May Allah be with you!'

Jaliram and Tandhan thanked him profusely and climbed the elephants that were decorated with heavy jewellery and velvet covers. The new additions made the *baarat* even more majestic.

'Abbu, why did you have to give them all this? Why be so gracious to them? They are our servants, so why make them look like kings?' Raj Kumar complained to his father.

Eyes narrowed, Jhadchand looked at the distant *baarat*.

'You are a fool!' He said. 'What you are seeing as my graciousness is merely an investment. He is a loyal servant, that too an intelligent and diligent one, and so is his son. They are emotional fools. Whatever you give them, they will return ten times. My gesture is an act of diplomacy to ensure that their loyalty remains with me. These acts are important to keep the flag of our rule flying over their lands. Let's go now, I am hungry. A feast awaits us.'

Dokwa

'How much you move! Stay still, Narayani', instructed Sheila. She was applying henna on Narayani's hand. Dipping a stick into the light green mix of henna, Sheila was making an image of a *dulhan*.

'You are marvellous, Sheila, your skill is outstanding. Only you can do this. But my friend, stop being so precise and hurry up! My back is hurting and I am losing patience, I can't stay still for so long', said Narayani.

'Don't listen to her, Sheila. Take your time and make the best design', said Ganga.

Just then, Ranjit walked in holding a bag of flowers

and announced that the *baarat* had left from Hisar and was going to reach there by late evening. 'I have cross-checked all the arrangements at the place of their stay twice.'

Meanwhile, Ganga and Gurshamal sat down for Ganesh puja to offer their prayers to the god of beginnings for a smooth and joyous wedding. Soon after, Gurshamal left to check if the streets were clean and the cooks had finished preparing sweets and the feast to be served to the *baaratis* at night.

'Don't worry, *tau*', said Ranjit, 'it's my sister's wedding, everything is taken care of and double-checked. Five boys will always be standing outside the place of stay for *baaratis* as guards. I will accompany the *baarat* on the way back myself.'

As Narayani waited for her *mehndi* to dry, everyone pampered her. They fed her sweets, helped her drink water, adjusted her *odhani*, and fulfilled her every wish.

'Aye Radha! Is your *dulha* coming to attend my wedding or not? He better come, ok?' Narayani said.

'Shhhh!' Radha blushed.

Cymbals, *shehnais*, and *dhols* announced the arrival of the *baarat*. Narayani's heart rate shot up suddenly. Looking at her *mehndi*, she blushed. Radha and Sheila got up, leaving the garlands they were preparing on the floor.

'Let's go and see the *dulha* and the *baarat*, I can't wait till tomorrow!'

'Sit down!' Lila said. 'Girls are not supposed to see

the *baarat*. It is bad manners. Stay indoors. Complete the garlands, there is still a lot of work left.'

'Let them go, Lila!' Ganga said. 'But look only from a distance, don't mingle with the *baaratis*. That would be considered rude. We have to serve them well, even a little slip here or there could create a scandal. Now go have fun but return soon.'

Ganga, whose heart was filled with varying emotions, looked at Narayani. Suddenly, her daughter's entire childhood started playing before her eyes and tears began to flow.

'Maa, it's my wedding, not *muklawa*, I will return in two days. Why are you crying?'

'They are tears of joy', explained Lila.

Until late in the night, music played in Ganga and Gurshamal's house, lanterns shone bright, and the entire courtyard and streets lined with festoons breathed life into the festivities. Piping hot dry fruit milk was served to beat the December chill. Everyone seemed to perpetually have their mouths full of sweets. Women sang songs and danced. Through their songs, they teased the bride, the groom, and the new family. The air lay thick with festivity.

In the other house, where the *baaratis* stayed, there were similar celebrations. The air was full of laughter and songs that *Jananis* sang to invoke their ancestors to send their blessings. They sang songs describing the celestial beauty of the bride and valour of the groom, and songs describing the love and affection of parents and relatives.

Kamal Ram and his gang of friends seated beside Tandhan could not stop praising the many beautiful girls they had spotted on their way.

'Gurshamal ji, your hospitality makes me feel like a king. Please sit down, I have not seen you take a breath since we arrived. My stomach is on the verge of bursting. Even then, my taste buds remain in denial, greedy to savour all your delicious delicacies. All this comfort and hospitality will make me a lazy man. Your arrangements are seriously spoiling us!' Jaliram said.

'He is certainly a very smart man', said Ranaji, still sulking.

Back in Ganga and Gurshamal's house, Radha nudged Narayani. 'Your *dulha* is so incredibly young and handsome! Surely the best this village has seen so far. You are so lucky, Narayani! If I wasn't married to my oldie, I would definitely marry the younger brother and come with you!'

'I was so awestruck by him that I failed to see the *dulha* altogether. Narayani, butter your mother-in-law and convince her to marry her younger son to me', said Geeta.

The friends gossiped and giggled all night. The guests left long after midnight. Gurshamal arrived home after everyone had left. His feet aching, his white *kurta* crumpled and stained, his hair a mess and his whole body falling apart in exhaustion when he sat down next to Narayani, he felt, for the first time that day, a surge of emotions. Until then, he'd had no time to process anything at all. He ran his hand over Narayani's forehead, tears trickling down.

'You surprise me so much! You are so strong and determined, challenging every situation, yet your heart is as gentle as any other woman's. We are truly blessed to have you in our life.'

Ganga wiped his tears and put a *kajal ka tikka* on Narayani's *mehndi*. 'May the colour of Tandhan's love never be drained from your hands!'

The dark colour of henna was symbolic of a husband's love for his wife. Everyone loved Narayani. All the men treated her as a sister and their wives pampered her. During the *haldi* ritual, all of Narayani's relatives and friends put a paste of *haldi* on her head, palms, and feet, blessing and offering gifts to her. The women later scrubbed her with *ubtan* made of curd, flour, turmeric, oil, and rose petals, and washed her hair with milk and curd to add sheen. Her beauty grew radiant not just because of it but also because of her love for Tandhan, which had finally been realised.

Sheila put her hair in a neat bun and decorated it with flowers. Ganga walked in holding the heavy wedding dress that had been stitched by the best tailor in Rajasthan with the golden zari work done by a renowned artist who weaved for the Mughal Sultanate. Her jewellery was exquisite, made by some of the most popular goldsmiths of the region.

The *mandap* for the *pheras* was decorated with marigold and rose flowers and had an *agni kund* (place to light the fire) in between. Panditji placed all the essentials needed for the ceremony next to it and started reciting *shlokas* to attract good energies and usher the gods to commence from heaven to bless the bride and groom.

Tandhan looked like a king dressed in a silver-gold sherwani with red zari work. His *bhabhis* adorned his eyes with *kajal*. Yamuna tied the *shera*, and his father, his heart bursting with pride, placed the *pagdi* firmly on Tandhan's head, symbolic of his esteem.

'Maa, if *bhaiya's* face will be covered by the *shera* at all times, how will *bhabhi* see his handsome face? And how will poor *bhaiya* see *bhabhi*?' Kamal said.

Yamuna pulled his ears. Tandhan was struck by Kamal's words. He was right, how will he see his beautiful bride? He longed to see Narayani. Heart bubbling with excitement, Tandhan mounted the mare. It was time to meet his bride. The *baarat* was huge. Men danced to the music of the *dhols*.

The energy of the procession was so electric that even gods would peep from heaven to take a look. Kamal Ram was at the forefront of celebrations along with friends, dancing like there was no tomorrow. Ladies followed the mare, dancing among themselves. Everyone stood outside their homes on the street, amazed by the grandeur of the procession. After hours of dance and merriment, the *baarat* reached Gurshamal's house.

Tandhan, with Kamal Ram on one side and his group of friends on the other, stood on the *choki* (low wooden stool) at the entrance of Narayani's house. Tandhan's heart longed for a glimpse of his bride. Ganga stood on the other side to welcome him with an *aarti thali*.

Women started singing songs about the arrival of the auspicious hour when the two would be tied by an inseparable knot for the rest of their lives. With a Neem twig, Tandhan hit the flower festoon tied on the entrance, symbolic of his arrival and stature. As Ganga dipped her finger in vermillion, he bowed low with grace. His friends teased him to stand tall and not bend. As he moved his *shera* to one side to allow Ganga to apply the *tikka*, he ran his eyes around the courtyard to spot his bride.

He saw her standing behind all the ladies, dressed in red, looking like a celestial nymph who had descended to the earth for him. Their eyes met and they both blinked together slowly as if to seal the vision of each other forever in their hearts. As he lowered his *shera*, Tandhan smiled, overwhelmed with a burgeoning feeling of love.

Masterji, who was going to perform the *pheras,* seated Tandhan in the *mandap* and began the Ganesh puja. Seeing Narayani's groom, he felt a great sense of pride and relief that his favourite disciple had found a worthy match. He called for Ganga and Gurshamal to be seated, and began the ritual of purity and preparation for the *Kanyadaan* (giving away the daughter in marriage).

Ganga's steps grew heavy walking towards the *mandap* as she remembered the seer's prediction. Gurshamal read her mind and came immediately to walk her to the *mandap*, holding her hand in a soothing manner. Narayani arrived with her veil drawn to her chin. She sat next to Tandhan on his left. Kamal Ram sat between them both.

'*Bhaiya*, think again; once married, there is no escape. You will have to dance to the tune of *bhabhi*. And even I won't be of help because from now on, I will serve her before you. So you better decide', teased Kamal.

Tandhan hit him with his elbow and Narayani giggled.

The two did the *jaimala* ceremony—exchanging garlands, symbolic of their choice of taking each other as their life partner. Tandhan then filled Narayani's *maang* (the middle parting of hair) with his blood, symbolising his commitment to uphold her honour even if it demanded his blood. He then put a *mangalsutra* around her neck, an auspicious thread in Hindu culture that signified a husband's love and promise that he would forever strive to keep his wife happy and protect her till his last breath.

Ganga and Gurshamal took a handful of money each, took Narayani's hand, and placed it in Tandhan's open palms, symbolising that from then onwards, their daughter belonged to him. Before the sacred fire, they gave their daughter away to him, which meant that from that point on, she would be led by her husband and her new family. Tears of love and joy flowed down Ganga and Gurshamal's faces as they completed the *Kanyadaan*, considered the highest of all *daans*—to give away one's own blood and flesh.

Masterji explained and made the two repeat the seven

vows of marriage—to build a family with strength, love, compassion, and honour, to be supportive of each other in doing so, to remain exceptionally loyal to each other and stand together in times of happiness and sorrows. Keeping the gods, the families, and the sacred fire as witnesses, they repeated the vows with conviction.

Masterji then asked them to stand up for the *pheras* around the fire. Ranjit stood between them, performing all the rites as a brother. He filled Narayani's hands with grains that she then put into the fire, symbolising his duty as a brother to always keep his sister's hands full of supplies. He then tied a knot between two pieces of cloth held by Narayani and Tandhan, ensuring that the knot was tight for it symbolised their bond. Masterji asked them to begin the *pheras*, led by Tandhan, and explained that from then on, Narayani vowed to follow and support her husband in all endeavours. After the completion of two circles around the fire, he then asked them to exchange places, making Narayani lead Tandhan.

He explained that in the event of such a situation arising when Tandhan could not lead the relationship, Narayani would step forward and take that place. With two *pheras* led by Tandhan and two by Narayani symbolising equality, their marriage was solemnised with vows of purity. Everyone showered flowers and wishes on the newlywed couple. The two sought everyone's blessings by touching their feet.

After the vows around the fire, Narayani's identity had shifted from being her parents' Laado to becoming the beloved wife of Tandhan. Ganga and Gurshamal suddenly felt alienated and lonely, as though their daughter was now no longer a part of their family but Jaliram's. The shift made the environment overwhelming.

Narayani's heart swelled with both happiness and sorrow. She rejoiced to have Tandhan, the man of her dreams, as her husband, but at the same time felt a profound sense of loss for now she no longer was Laado to her parents, friends, and the village. Suddenly, everything appeared foreign. Realising her state of mind, Tandhan quietly held her hand and squeezed it for her to know that he understood and he was there with her in this emotional time.

To ease the ambience, the jokes began. Tandhan started by reciting poetry and *shlokas* to tease the ladies of the village and to praise his mother-in-law. Everyone laughed and the air soon filled with joy.

At dinner, following the ritual, Gurshamal graciously seated the members of Tandhan's family before beautiful *Chokis* with *thals* (big metal dinner plates) filled with delicacies. Gurshamal, Ganga and all the relatives served them and fed them with honour. After dinner, Ranjit carried an empty vessel and Radha poured water to wash their hands. Gurshamal followed after them and gifted each member gold coins. Standing with his hands joined before Jaliram, Gurshamal said, 'Jaliramji, I hope our conduct and hospitality have been satisfying. If we have erred or made a mistake in any matter, please forgive us!' He then moved to remove his own *pagdi* to place before him.

Jaliram immediately stopped him from removing his headgear and held both his hands in his. 'Gurshamal ji, please don't do this! I am completely against this ritual. You have served us to our hearts' content, given us memories to last an entire lifetime and, above all, given us your precious daughter. We do not need or deserve anything more. And let me also tell you this, in Narayani, we have been gifted a daughter by the Lord today. We will do everything to keep her happy, just like you have done all these years!'

It was almost dawn and time for the bride's *vidaai* (departure). With tears in their eyes, Ganga and her friends prepared her for the journey. Narayani dipped her hands in vermillion water and left her handprints on the wall, then one by one hugged everyone, sobbing on their shoulders. Gurshamal held her face and looked at it for a long time, reliving every single moment from her birth till that point.

'Laado, I am a very proud father, now make them proud too, with your love and devotion. May Lord Narayan bless you, *bitiya*.'

Narayani clung to him and did not let go until Radha and Sheila cajoled her. Wiping her tears, Ganga stayed strong. 'It's just a matter of two days. Stay happy and keep everyone happy, my child!'

Juggli kept moving her legs and making her anklets chime to get Narayani's attention. Narayani took a bundle of grass and fed her while running a loving hand over her back. Led by Tandhan, they stepped outside the house. Narayani turned to look back. Along with Ranjit, Gurshamal seated her in the *doli* adorned with flowers and filled with nuts, fruits, and *sharbat* bottles for the journey. He ran a loving hand over her head.

'Ranjit is coming along and will bring you back in two days' time. Take care, *bitiya*, and be obedient and loving to your new family. Receive and give compassion and love.'

Holding the reins of the golden brown horse that he had bought from the Arab trader a few weeks back, Gurshamal handed it to Tandhan. 'Take this gift, *beta*. Ride back home on this. It's a superior breed horse that shall complement your riding skills.'

Tandhan touched his feet. 'Thank you, baba! But what was the need for this? You have already given us so much.'

'Take it as a gift from a father to a son.'

Tandhan beamed looking at the horse, for it was just the kind he always wanted. In one jump, he mounted it and patted it on the neck, forming a bond. Led by Ranaji, Tandhan, and other security men, the procession began moving. Narayani's *doli* and carts filled with gifts were at the centre of the procession followed by Jaliram, Kamal Ram, and Ranjit and his men at the end.

Gurshamal and Ganga stood watching, reciting the Lord's name for the safe journey of their Laado and her new family.

Seated in the *doli*, Narayani's heart ached and longed for her parents. She suddenly felt alienated, surrounded by new faces. She longed for a familiar face. Remembering Ranjit *bhaiya*, she pulled the curtain and peeped outside to look at him. On seeing Narayani search for someone, Tandhan dismounted his horse and walked towards her *doli*. Ranjit had also reached her but on seeing Tandhan, he smiled and stepped back, happy to see the gesture of care.

Tandhan pulled back the curtain. On seeing Tandhan instead of Ranjit *bhaiya*, Narayani jolted upright from her slouching posture and immediately pulled down her veil. Her heart raced and her hands began to sweat.

'Do you need anything?' Tandhan asked.

Mesmerised as always by his voice, she nodded.

His eyes fell on her feet, painted with henna, anklets resting on top of the deep brown colour—a stark contrast to her fair skin—and the ring on her second toe.

'Is that a cockroach there?' He pointed in the corner.

She immediately removed her veil. 'Eew, where? Where?'

Tandhan laughed heartily.

She looked at him and smiled, then overcome with shyness, she slowly pulled down her *ghunghat*. Her cheeks burnt with the intense rush of blood.

Tandhan extended his hand and picked up an apple. He took a bite of it and then looked at the veiled face of Narayani. 'You are very beautiful.' He then handed her the apple. 'You must be hungry.'

Narayani took the apple and chewed on it. Tandhan's presence had a calming effect on her and eased her anxiety. After spending time with him, she felt safe and relaxed. Tandhan went back to his position and Narayani fell asleep in her *doli*. She was home.

CHAPTER 17

Homecoming

'They are here! THEY ARE HERE!'

Fixing her *odhani*, Yamuna crossed the room in a couple of strides. She joined the other women in watching the men lower the *doli*. The moment it touched the ground, she rushed forward and like a mother lifts her baby, she lifted Narayani in her arms and escorted the bride. While the other women sang songs about the new bride's arrival, Yamuna welcomed the bride and groom with an *aarti thali*. Reciting the lord's name and holding Tandhan's hand, Narayani stepped into the house by first placing her right foot inside.

Kamal Ram and his female cousins stopped the newlywed couple.

'First, our gift. Without one, we won't let you enter the house.'

Jaliram and Yamuna showered the youngsters with gold coins. The couple stepped inside and paid reverence, at first to Lord Shiva and then their family ancestors, for a blissful married life. Narayani, her face covered in a veil, looked around her new home. The courtyard, painted a bright orange, had a buffalo and two cows. The entire house was big and airy and nothing like the old one where she grew up. At last, Yamuna took her to the kitchen where she sought Goddess Annapurna's blessings.

Next began the age-old tradition of testing the new bride for various qualities through a series of games. In a bowl of coloured water, Tandhan and Narayani were put to the task of finding a ring in it. Family members cheered as the two tried to trace the ring and they broke into applause as the two found the ring at the same time. Next, Narayani was asked to pick metal plates without making any noise, a task she was able to finish with remarkable speed and accuracy. One by one, she finished every task with precision and agility. Everyone was growing restless to see her face.

To begin the ritual of *muhdikhai* (unveiling the face), she was seated on a *choki* (low wooden stool) with her *ghunghat* drawn over her face. Jaliram was the first to step ahead and lift the veil.

'My daughter is absolutely beautiful! Welcome home, *bahurani*!' He said, his voice choking with emotions.

One by one, everyone lifted her veil and grew mesmerised by her beauty.

'Will *bhaiya* get a chance or not? Poor *bhaiya*, he has been trying hard to steal a glimpse of his bride', said Kamal Ram.

Tandhan glared at Kamal Ram, then walked into the kitchen.

'Where are you going?'

'I am thirsty, I need to drink some water.'

'If by thirsty you mean embarrassed then water is not the solution', said Kamal Ram.

Narayani blushed as everyone else burst out laughing.

'Congratulations, Jaliram!'

Jhadchand walked into the house with his son Raj Kumar. Everyone stood up, surprised and unprepared for the Nawab's visit. He had never stepped into a commoner's house.

'Hearing about your safe arrival and your remarkable daughter-in-law, I could not resist coming here to bless them.' He turned to his servants and nodded. Immediately, they stepped forward with massive *thaals* in their hands covered with gifts.

Tandhan and Narayani touched his feet to seek his blessings. Jaliram then offered him a seat and refreshments.

'Thank you, Jaliram! But you know my taste buds are fussy…'

Raj Kumar nudged Tandhan with a naughty smile and congratulated him. As the father and son climbed on their elephant to return, Raj Kumar caught a glimpse of Tandhan's new golden-brown horse tied in the stable.

'I have never seen a horse of such remarkable strength, height, and beauty. Don't you think, *Abbu*?'

'Hmph.' Jhadchand, immersed in making a grand show of his power to the villagers who had gathered to see him, did not so much as look at the horse. Raj Kumar continued to stare at the horse, obsessed. On reaching the palace, he summoned the minister and instructed him to order a horse just like Tandhan's.

Meanwhile, exhausted after a long day of rituals and entertaining guests, the family sat down for dinner. For Narayani, this was a significant moment for she was sharing her first meal with her new family. She sat beside Yamuna, covered in a veil, as Yamuna served *chapattis* to them.

'Maa ji, allow me to make rotis. You must be tired', spoke Narayani, her voice a mere whisper.

Yamuna ran a loving hand over her head.

'No *bitiya*, you are still quite young and here only for a day. When you grow up and return after the *muklawa*, I will hand over all responsibilities to you.'

Tandhan and Kamal Ram fed Yamuna a bite before they started eating. Moved by the brothers' gesture that showed clearly their love for Yamuna, Narayani fell deeper in love with her husband. She observed Tandhan as he went about the house, took mental notes of his every little gesture and expression; the way he lifted the *lota* of water and washed his hands, and the meticulous manner in which he folded his mat and put it back in place.

'Eat, *bitiya*! You are not eating anything', said Yamuna.

After the men finished dinner and got up, the two sat down to eat at last. Although Narayani was starving, she struggled to eat with the veil. Realising this, Yamuna put down her morsel and lifted Narayani's *ghunghat*.

'You can relax and be the way you would be at your parents' house. The guests and your *baba* have left.'

Narayani took her first bite and immediately looked at Yamuna. 'Maa ji, you cook very tasty food. You must teach me too.'

'Bhabhi!' Kamal Ram walked in. 'Leave some room in your stomach. I have brought your favourite *boondi*.'

Narayani looked at him and smiled. He served it on her plate and left to attend to the horses.

'*Bhaiya!* I forgot to give treats to the horses, could you please bring the pack of *boondi* from the kitchen?' Kamal Ram asked.

Tandhan rushed into the house and just as he entered the kitchen, he saw Narayani's lovely face without any hindrance from the *odhani*. She stopped chewing and turned pink. By the time he had picked up the *boondi* packet, Kamal Ram had come back to the kitchen.

'You can thank me for this', he whispered into Tandhan's ear, 'by letting me ride your new horse!'

The two headed back to the stable with the *boondi*.

After finishing dinner, Yamuna spread a bedsheet on the charpoy next to her for Narayani. Jaliram returned from his routine evening stroll and announced his arrival by clearing his throat. Narayani quickly pulled down her veil so that it covered her face yet again and stood behind Yamuna like a shadow.

'Take this home as yours, *bitiya*', said Jaliram, 'do not hesitate to ask for anything. Yamuna is like your mother and I, your father.'

Holding her by the hand, Yamuna made Narayani stand in front of Jaliram. She then adjusted her veil and raised it from her chin to her head.

'Think of him as your father. You need not cover your whole face, this much is enough to convey respect.'

Just then, Kamal entered the room.

'Maa, baba, since *bhabhi* will go back tomorrow, can I show her around the house?'

'Of course!'

The two were about to head out when Ranaji walked in.

'Where is Tandhan? We have to discuss things for tomorrow…'

Seeing Narayani's unveiled face, he changed the subject. 'I can see the value system of this house changing rapidly…'

'Ranaji', said Kamal, 'take it easy! After all, you are getting old. And please spare *bhaiya* from work for a day at least. Let's go, *bhabhi*!'

Narayani followed Kamal to the shed. There, running his hand over the cow, he introduced her to Narayani. 'She is Amba, the eldest one.'

Narayani beamed and ran a hand over its back. 'What a coincidence! We have a cow by the same name! What's the name of the other one there?'

'Other introductions can wait, *bhabhi*', whispered Kamal. '*Bhaiya* is waiting in the stable, he wants to meet you. Follow me.'

Narayani followed, biting down the smile on her lips.

Tandhan stood next to his new horse, fidgeting with the lantern. From the corner of his eyes, he saw the two approaching. Feigning ignorance, he continued to adjust the lantern, lowering its flame. Clearing his throat loudly, Kamal retreated. Removing her *odhani*, Narayani walked towards Tandhan as he continued to adjust the lantern. Unable to exercise restraint, Tandhan finally turned around with a handsome smile on his lips. Narayani stopped and smiled back, then immediately lowered her eyes. Tandhan took a step forward to bridge the gap between them. Her ability to transform from a fierce warrior to a woman oozing with feminine grace didn't fail to mesmerise Tandhan.

'Why did you call me?' She asked in mock anger.

'I called you? Kamal said it was you who called me to meet!'

They teased each other.

Narayani stepped forward to run her hand across the neck of the horse.

'He is beautiful, isn't he?'

Tandhan started stroking its neck too.

'He certainly is.'

Their hands brushed against each other and Narayani retracted hers immediately. Stepping forward, Tandhan reached for her hand and squeezed it tight. Narayani could not look at him, her insides melting away. Tandhan's eyes gorged on her beauty; her eyes holding entire universes within them, her pink lips soft and trembling, her cheeks flushed. Never before had either experienced such a surge of love within them.

'I still haven't seen you or spoken to you enough, and you are leaving tomorrow. Isn't this unfair?'

She nodded. 'It's only a matter of time, then every second of my every day for the rest of my life shall be ours. For now, these precious few memories should sustain us till we meet again, my dearest.'

Tandhan stroked her cheek with the back of his hand. Just then, they heard Kamal approaching the stable. The two hastily stepped away from each other. Narayani covered her head and turned to return to the house. Tandhan stood next to his horse in a daze, watching her walk away, longing to hold Narayani in his arms.

Back in the house, Narayani lay down on the *charpoy* next to Yamuna, her heart still beating rapidly. She looked across to the courtyard where Tandhan slept beside Kamal. In the dim light, she kept gazing at him. Reliving that moment when he had held her hand she fell asleep eventually.

At dawn, Yamuna patted Narayani's forehead.

'*Bitiya*! Freshen up and get dressed before the men wake up. I will prepare breakfast and pack food for the journey.'

Tandhan stirred, hearing the sound of Narayani's anklets. He had barely slept, determined to spend as much time as he could with Narayani on her last day there.

Meanwhile, Yamuna helped the little bride dress up.

'*Bitiya*, you are the pride and honour of our family now. Take good care of yourself back home till Tandhan comes to pick you up on *muklawa*.'

Narayani touched her feet and headed towards the bullock cart that had been filled with necessary supplies for her journey back to Dokwa from Hisar. Ranjit and his two horsemen prepared to leave. She touched Tandhan and Jaliram's feet and waved to Kamal. Biding her new family farewell, Narayani climbed the cart with a heavy heart, surprised at how quickly this house and family had become hers. Just as the cart was about to leave, Ranaji arrived.

'These five men shall accompany you, Ranjitji, for safety', he said.

Seeing Ranaji, Narayani got down and, lowering her *odhani*, touched his feet.

'*Akhand saubhagyawati bhava!* Take care and travel safe.'

'What's the need for more horsemen? We will be safe', said Ranjit.

'Her safety is paramount to us...they will drop her and return, it is no trouble.'

Long after the carts left, Tandhan stood watching.

'Let's get to work now', said Ranaji.

Embarrassed, Tandhan nodded and headed inside to get dressed.

A Death

Mounting his new horse, whom he had named Pavan, Tandhan entered the *akhara* for daily practice. Raj Kumar, who was practising with the sword, saw the horse and turned green with envy. While Tandhan was tying the horse, Raj Kumar walked towards him, his eyes on the beast.

'This beauty and strength do not suit your stature. It is meant for royalty like me. Let me show you.'

He leapt to mount the horse. Neighing, the horse jumped, throwing Raj Kumar on the ground.

Tandhan patted the horse and it calmed down immediately. 'He knows its master. They choose well', he said. He stretched his hand towards Raj Kumar. 'Let's resume our practice', he said.

Raj Kumar was furious. He had always gotten what he wanted. 'How about a friendly sword duel between me and Tandhan? I am tired of solo practice', he proposed to Ranaji.

He agreed.

The two picked up their swords and stood facing each other, Ranaji between them. Before Ranaji could signal them to start, Raj Kumar placed a heavy blow on Tandhan's sword. Both Ranaji and Tandhan understood immediately that this was anything but a friendly duel. He kept attacking Tandhan with unprecedented aggression. Tandhan maintained his calm throughout and only defended himself, never once attacking him. Ranaji, who understood both Raj Kumar's immaturity and Tandhan's ability to handle any situation, chose not to intervene.

'Easy *Bhaaya*! It's just a practice session, not a fight!' Tandhan spoke.

Raj Kumar had turned deaf. His attacks grew more and more brutal. If he wanted, Tandhan could end the duel in a minute but he chose not to. With a vicious blow, Raj Kumar cut Tandhan on his left arm.

'Careful, Tandhan! Attack!' Ranaji yelled, realising that Raj Kumar would not hesitate to kill Tandhan.

Tandhan's demeanour changed from friend to foe. It was time to show Raj Kumar who was really in control. Within minutes, Raj Kumar was on the floor, his sword out of his reach. Jhadchand, who was on his usual vigilance rounds, applauded.

'Bravo, Tandhan! Exemplary skills! Ranaji, you have trained him well. Raj Kumar has a good team to serve him.' He then turned towards his son. 'Raj Kumar, come along to the court. Some traders are waiting to meet you.'

Back at the court, Raj Kumar's rage turned to fury. 'This is trash! You call them horses? They are worse than mares! Fit to carry loads and bear foals. I need a horse that suits my stature; hot-blooded, strong, and handsome.' Raj Kumar spat at the traders who had gathered to display their horses.

Jhadchand waved his hand. Everyone left the court barring Jhadchand and his son.

'What is the matter, Raj? You seem rather annoyed. These were some of the finest horses from across the subcontinent. Do you have any particular horse in mind? Tell me! There is nothing I can't get my son.'

'Have you seen Tandhan's horse, *abbu*? Its skin resembles gold...it towers above all other horses...it doesn't run, it flies. It could defeat a lion with childish ease, what strength it holds in its muscles! And you say these are the finest horses? I want Tandhan's horse, *abbu*!'

Jhadchand laughed. 'So much fury for such a petty thing! I shall buy it for you today itself. You shouldn't waste your emotions on such things, Raj. Go and pamper yourself with a massage and some wine. You will have the horse tomorrow.'

Later that evening, Jaliram and his family sat down for dinner. To everyone's surprise, Jaliram fed the first morsel to Tandhan.

'What is it that you want, baba? You can demand it right away.' Tandhan laughed.

Pushing away his plate of food, Jaliram looked at his son. 'Beta, I heard about the incident at the *akhara*...the

Nawab has quoted a sum of 200 gold coins for Pavan. Raj Kumar wishes to buy it', he spoke in a subdued tone.

'But we did not put it up for sale!' Kamal and Tandhan spoke in chorus.

'How then does the question of buying arise?' Tandhan asked. 'I will go to the palace right now and decline the offer! It is my most precious gift and I will never sell it no matter how good the price.'

Tandhan pushed away his plate and got up.

'Sit down!' said Jaliram. 'I will handle it.'

The next day, Jaliram explained to Jhadchand that it was considered inauspicious and disrespectful to sell a gift received from one's in-laws. Knowing that Jaliram was integral to the administrative body, Jhadchand chose to let go of the demand. He gifted two huge elephants and four horses to Raj Kumar instead. Realising that his father had to be diplomatic, Raj Kumar approached Tandhan directly and offered him double the original price. Even before Raj Kumar could complete phrasing the offer, Tandhan politely refused and walked away.

Dokwa

'You are beautiful!' Narayani could hear Tandhan speak as she finished filling her *maang* with *sindoor*. She then lifted her *jhola*, ready to go to school.

'Laado', said Gurshamal, 'sit down, I want to tell you something.'

'Yes, baba?'

'You were my responsibility until the *pheras* took

place. Now, you are Tandhan's wife and your respect and honour are attached to his family and him. You must step into this new identity now and forego the previous one. Till the time of *muklawa*, you have to stop going to school and the *akhara, bitiya*.'

She nodded in compliance. 'You are right, baba. I understand.' Putting aside her *jhola*, she went to the kitchen. 'Maa, I am going to Gangu *halwai's* shop, I will be back before dusk.'

'Gangu *halwai*! What for? Your father bought *laddoos* yesterday, they are still in stock. How many more do you want to eat?' Ganga said.

'I know, *maa*, I am not going there to buy *laddoos*.'
'Then?'

'I am going to learn how to make *mirchi vada*. I will go now. I shall come back and cook for you and *baba*.'

'*Mirchi vada*! Now she wants to become a *halwai*? I fail to understand this girl. Her in-laws are going to have a very difficult time with her!' Mumbling, Ganga resumed her work.

At the *halwai*, Narayani quickly got to work.

'You are a quick learner, *bitiya*! Even I can't fry them with such consistent colour. And the slight sweetness you added makes the potato stuffing taste even better. You surely have Annapurna's magical hands', said Gangu *halwai*.

As soon as Narayani took a bite, her eyes filled with tears and her nose turned red. To douse the internal fire, she tossed a *laddoo* in her mouth. 'You really think they are nice, Gangu *tau*? Will anyone actually enjoy eating these?'

'You have a sweet tooth, *bitiya*. That's why you don't savour it the way I do. Anyone who loves spicy food will ask for a second helping of it. You are good enough to open your own shop.'

Reassured by Gangu's words, Narayani prepared them at home. Her parents loved it. Ganga insisted that she take some to the neighbours too.

'Wow! Did you really prepare them, *laado*? They look as though they are made by a *halwai*', said Lila.

'You know, *maa*, *mirchi vada* is her husband's favourite', said Radha, taking a bite.

Narayani blushed.

'She is sweet and he is spicy, what a mouth-watering combination!'

Narayani pinched her. 'I should go now, it's getting late.'

With every passing day, Narayani was easing into her new role and life.

'You have never done it before. Leave it, I will do it.' Ganga stopped Narayani as the latter tried to take over her task of grinding wheat in the *chakki* (a grinding machine made with two circular heavy stones).

'You still doubt my strength! I will grind them all today itself', said Narayani.

Ganga protested but Narayani refused to relent. Giving up, Ganga went into the kitchen. She returned an hour later and, to her surprise, found that Narayani had kept her promise. Though she had never ground wheat in a *chakki* before, a rather tedious task, she managed to finish grinding more than a kilo in one go.

'Your mother-in-law is blessed to have found you! She will surely become fat once you go there.'

'This is all because of Ghanshyam *tau's* rigorous training', said Narayani as she filled *aata* in the brass container.

In the days that followed, she learnt to apply *mehndi* from Sheila. Keen to give her house a makeover, she asked Gurshamal to bring coloured dyes from Bhiwani on his trade trip. She then painted the walls of their house with flowers and dainty butterflies in vibrant hues, similar to those at Tandhan's house. Gurshamal and Ganga were happy to see the grace with which their little Laado had assumed a new identity and persona.

'I don't know what good deeds I performed in my previous birth that Lord Vishnu gave me a daughter like her!'

Hisar

Raj Kumar's begum appeared in front of him holding a silver tray. On it was a silver glass filled with a red drink. 'Try this new drink I prepared by grinding dry fruits with fresh rose petals. It will cool you down and induce a good night's sleep', she said.

As Raj Kumar flung his hand, the tray and the glass smashed into the wall. 'GET OUT! I need no *sharbats* or empty talks to soothe me. Leave me alone, sleep in the kid's chambers. LEAVE RIGHT NOW!'

Picking up the distorted glass, she walked away. 'Hell with him and his father.'

Raj Kumar kept pacing in his chamber. He even declined his father's invitation to join him for dinner. Till midnight, he lay awake.

'My friendship and politeness have been taken for granted and perceived as my weakness. If Tandhan can have the audacity to decline a Nawab's offer, he has to face the brunt. That horse has filled him with unnecessary pride and ego. It's time he loses it. If not by request, then by force I shall possess that horse. Once I tie it in my stable, let me see how he will take it back. There are no laws for Nawabs.'

He changed his attire and covered his face to look like an ordinary villager, and then left the palace in disguise at night. The streets were empty. Even the stray dogs had dozed off. Raj Kumar jumped over the wall of Tandhan's house. Making sure that no one was around watching him, he slipped inside the stable. Sensing a foreign presence, Pavan began to neigh and move restlessly.

Being a light sleeper, Tandhan's eyes opened immediately. He could now hear Pavan jumping. A stray animal had entered the stable, he was quite sure. Picking up the *bhaala* resting beside him on the *charpoy*, he rushed towards the stable.

Seeing a shadow move next to Pavan, he threw the *bhaala* in its direction with all his might.

'Argh!'

Surprised to hear a human voice, he reached to light the lantern. Pavan stopped neighing. As the light of the lantern cut through the darkness, Tandhan saw the person lying dead in front of him and stumbled backwards in horror. Jaliram and Kamal, who had reached the spot by then, let out a collective gasp. Jaliram fell to his knees.

'What have you done, you fool!'

'I…I thought it was an animal…I didn't mean to…I didn't know it was Raj Kumar. Trust me, baba, it was an accident! This would have never happened if I knew. I…I am so sorry!' Tandhan sobbed.

Kamal turned and rushed to call Ranaji. Jaliram stepped forward and wiped his son's tears. 'What's done is done. This is no time to lament. Jhadchand will turn this house into a pool of bodies. We have to leave the town immediately before the village awakens.'

Ranaji, who had now joined them, agreed. 'He will definitely not spare anyone. We have to leave…but where will we go?'

'Jhunjhunu!' Jaliram said promptly. 'It's only 130 km away. The administrator is my good friend and has invited me there several times. His relationship with Jhadchand is anything but cordial. Besides, he overpowers him in strength and position. We will be safe there. Let's leave immediately!'

'Kamal, you ride on my horse with me, Yamuna bhabhi with Tandhan. Mount the weapons on Jaliramji's horse', said Ranaji.

Jaliram looked at Ranaji in confusion.

'What will I do here without my family? If we stay, I stay. If we leave, I leave', said Ranaji.

Jaliram stepped forward and hugged him.

Leaving behind all their belongings, the family left immediately and crossed the village territory before dawn.

Meanwhile, at the palace, Jhadchand was growing furious by the minute.

'What do you mean no one has seen him since last night? Go call Shabana, she will know where he is', he roared.

When Shabana too denied knowing anything about Raj Kumar's whereabouts, Jhadchand grew suspicious. He commanded all his guards to search for Raj Kumar in every corner of the palace.

In the village, Jaliram's neighbours were growing curious too. The house sat unusually quiet and no one seemed to be home. Vimla stepped into the house to check. 'Yamuna! Yamuna! Where are you? *Bhaaya*! Tandhan!'

When there was no response, she started searching the house. Finding no one, she stood wondering where the entire family could have gone so early in the morning. Just then, she heard the cows mooing. Realising that she had not checked there, she went to the stable. There, on seeing Raj Kumar's body, she let out a horrified scream. Soon, the entire village gathered and shivered in fear on seeing the dead body of the Nawab's son. Word reached the palace.

'What do you mean you don't know? You live next door and you say that you don't know what happened and where they have gone?'

In the palace court, the entire village had gathered. Jhadchand was livid.

Just then, a guard arrived. 'An old man saw the family leave town before dawn. We have reason to believe that they have moved to our opponent's territory of Jhunjhunu.'

Jhadchand raised his hand. Immediately, everyone left. Raj Kumar's body lay in front of him. When Shabana entered the court with her children, all of them dressed in white and sobbing uncontrollably, Jhadchand nearly collapsed on his throne.

'Ya Allah! How do I bear this sight and the pain that has shattered my heart? My inability to fulfil my son's desire has led to this. How will I ever forgive myself? How will I ever bring back the smiles on my daughter-in-law's and grandchildren's faces?'

As tears washed his grief, fury began to rise.

'TANDHAN! Your head at my feet shall be the ointment for my wounds. Only your blood will cleanse it, nothing else. Hide wherever you want, my sword will track you and smear itself with your blood', he screamed in pain. Jhadchand placed his hand on Shabana's head. 'Weep not, my daughter! I know your loss is irreplaceable but I will bring Tandhan's wife to serve you as a slave for the rest of her life. This is your Abbu's promise and a Nawab's resolve.'

CHAPTER 19

Jhunjhunu

The lush green fields, smooth and clean roads, well-built houses, and bustling markets indicated two things—Jhunjhunu's prosperity and an able administrator at the helm.

With the sun, now exactly overhead, the family had finally entered the town. They had been moving non-stop since they left home. Their clothes were covered in dust, their throats were parched, and their stomachs churned in perpetual fear; the family was on the verge of an emotional breakdown.

Villagers looked at them with curiosity and suspicion. 'Where is the Nawab's palace?' Ranaji asked.

One of the villagers pointed them in the direction they were already heading. The family continued moving and reached the gates half an hour later. Jaliram dismounted the horse, every bone in his body hurting after the long journey. He asked the gatekeeper to inform the Nawab of his arrival.

Everyone got down from their horses. While Ranaji stood behind Jaliram, Tandhan, and Kamal looked around the new town. Their hearts longed for the comfort of their home and the familiarity of their town. Yamuna stood beside Tandhan, her covered head resting on his shoulder, tired from the long journey and emotionally overwhelmed by the turn of events. Overnight, they had lost everything—their home, town, belongings, everything.

After a few minutes, the Diwan himself came to the door to escort Jaliram, a gesture befitting the latter's reputation. With tremendous respect, he ushered them in and listened with patience to the events of the previous night as recounted by them. After contemplating for a while, he asked his servants to escort them to the guest chamber.

'Jaliramji, I have much respect for you and your work…and I deeply grieve the circumstances. Fear no more, you are in our territory now. The enemy's hand can never reach you. For now, you must all rest. I will meet you tomorrow at the court. I have called for an emergency meeting.'

The family heaved a sigh of relief. As they collapsed on the bed, tears started flowing. Ranaji remained immune to the emotional outburst. At the moment, the family's safety was his only concern. Although he did not say anything to Jaliram, he suspected the Nawab's intention. Why had he summoned a court meeting? A paranoid Ranaji suspected foul play.

Next morning, while Yamuna stayed in the chamber, Jaliram, Ranaji, Tandhan, and Kamal dressed in the clothes they were offered and left for the court. Ranaji carried his sword with him and urged Kamal and Tandhan to do the same.

'Why carry weapons to court? It makes a bad impression. He is a trustworthy man!' Jaliram said.

'Under current circumstances, it is better to take the necessary precautions than to blindly trust. I don't understand; why is he being so nice?'

Jaliram shook his head and decided not to argue further.

'I hope you all slept well', said the Nawab. 'You are safe here, and no deceit shall meet you! Your enemy has always been my enemy. It is a long story...I have old scores to settle with him, which I am certain you can help me do. After all, you have worked with him for so long.'

Ranaji eased for the first time since his arrival and placed his sword aside. The court commenced and the Nawab introduced Jaliram as the new assistant Diwan of the town. He introduced him to members of the court who would assist him with work and informed the servants to take the family to their new home that had been prepared for them.

'I don't have words to thank you, my friend. I shall serve you till my last breath', said Jaliram, bowing down in gratitude.

Filled with hope and joy, the family moved into the new home. Although smaller than their previous home, everyone loved it for it felt warm and safe. Together with a guard, they explored the whole town. The family made acquaintance with locals and their new neighbours.

Later that night at dinner, as Tandhan took the first morsel, he broke down into tears. He got up immediately and went outside. Kamal followed.

'It's all my fault. If I had not killed Raj Kumar, we would be in our home, our town. I am the reason for all this misery!' Tandhan sobbed.

'No *bhaiya*! It is not your fault. That scoundrel had come to steal Pavan. And what happened was an accident. Had I been in your place, I would have done the same thing.'

Tandhan shook his head. 'I killed a human being!'

Ranaji had followed them out too. He placed a hand on Tandhan's shoulder. 'Tandhan, I know your heart. Your sword never kills, it only defends. It was his misdeed that brought him his death. You threw your weapon at him thinking that it was a predator. Stop punishing yourself with this guilt', said Ranaji.

Tandhan continued to sob.

'And as Lord Shiva has rightfully said, everyone's death is pre-written, we are just mediums for it. Your weapon was chosen by the Lord to punish and kill him. You have no reason to repent!' Jaliram said, also having come out to console his son. 'Maa is upset, come and have dinner. From now on, nobody is ever going to talk about this episode. It's in the past, leave it behind.'

Over the new few days, the family warmed up to

their new home. The people of Jhunjhunu were a happy and prosperous lot. They embraced the new family with open arms. The locals, a religious and faithful bunch, were ruled by a kind and compassionate leader. Unlike Jhadchand, he served his people with love and not fear and dominance. He had built a strong community that stood united in times of crisis. No neighbouring Mughal had ever even tried to trespass into their area for the people of Jhunjhunu were extremely loyal to their leader and would do anything for him.

Hisar

Jhadchand struck the man with his whip yet again.

'I need details of the whole incident! Speak up, you moron.'

The lean man whimpered in pain. 'My lord, it was late at night. We were fast asleep so we did not hear any noise. In the morning, when my wife did not see the family, she went to check the house. If not for her, we would have never known a thing, my lord. We know nothing.'

'Then who does? Who else is involved in the conspiracy of my beloved son's death?'

Jhadchand lashed the man with his whip once more.

A guard stepped forward just then. 'My lord, there is no conspiracy. We assessed the whole place...it is quite clear that Kumar had gone to steal the horse. No sword was used, and there was no duel. From the way he died, it seems that one of the family members threw the spear at him in the dark…to shoo away the thief. Kumar got hit by the spear and died.'

Jhadchand looked at his strongest guards and nodded. They grabbed the man and pulled him into the next chamber. He let out a scream and then fell silent.

'What is the purpose of a tongue that does not know its rightful use?' Jhadchand said to the court filled with scared souls. 'Make an announcement in this village and all the neighbouring ones—whoever brings me a member of the family alive will receive a sack of gold coins as a reward. Appoint a spy to keep a constant watch on them. I will have the rats come out of their hole soon! Only once my sword is dipped in their blood will I sleep in peace.'

Dokwa

Narayani's flesh broke into goosebumps as she read the letter from Jaliram that her father received from a trader. In it, he narrated the entire episode leading up to Kumar's death and the family's overnight migration to Jhunjhunu. Her heart ached to reach out to Tandhan in these trying times. Before the trader could return, Narayani parcelled a pack of *Mirchi vada* along with a letter to be delivered to Tandhan. Just as the trader was about to leave, Gurshamal stopped him.

'Wait *Bhaaya!* I shall join you.'

Gurshamal looked at Ganga and Narayani. 'The family has been through a lot. I shall go and meet Jaliramji. They are family now.'

On the way to Jhunjhunu, Gurshamal was reminded of the seer's words about Tandhan's early death. It was only when he met the family and saw them safe and happy in Jhunjhunu that he heaved a sigh of relief. He said a silent prayer thanking Lord Vishnu for saving his son-in-law from what appeared to be certain death.

Jhunjhunu

Kamal looked on with curiosity as Tandhan unwrapped the parcel sent by Narayani. He grabbed a *Mirchi vada* immediately.

'*Bhaiya*, sharing is caring!' Kamal said. Grabbing a second one, he ran to Yamuna. 'Maa, taste these, the best I have eaten till date. *Bhabhi* prepared them. I can't wait to try the rest of her cooking.'

Relishing the *vada*, Tandhan opened the letter. The writing was smeared in several places from what he understood was Narayani's tears. Pain and anxiety were written all over the letter. 'Can't wait to come home to you!' Tandhan read aloud the last line in the letter. He looked up at the sky wistfully. 'Even I can't wait to have you here. I miss the memories of you at the old house. Come soon and make some here now.'

CHAPTER 20

Muklawa

Dokwa

Curled in a foetal position, Narayani moaned in pain. Her mother gave her a glass of turmeric milk to drink. When that too failed to ease the pain, she went to sleep pressing a small earthen pot filled with warm ash against her abdomen. The next morning, she woke up to find crimson stains all over her *ghaghra*. Immediately, she ran to her mother.

'Maa, what are these stains on my clothes? I am certain I did not hurt myself. Is this some kind of disease? Am I going to die?'

Ganga saw the stains and explained to her that she was entering a new phase of growth and transformation. 'It is time for Laado's *Muklawa*', she told Gurshamal.

'But only eight months have passed since her wedding!'

'She is *ready…*'

'I will go to Panditji tomorrow then…find out an auspicious time for her *vidaai*.'

Ganga looked around their house with wet eyes. 'It is time to prepare for an empty nest.'

Gurshamal nodded. 'I have to visit Jhunjhunu for business, I will leave early morning.'

The next morning, as Gurshamal prepared to set off for the journey, Ganga handed him the *jhola* he always carried with him. 'Your trade visits to Jhunjhunu have increased…are you setting up a business there so that you can meet your Laado more often in the future?'

Gurshamal left without replying and headed straight to Panditji's house. He came home later that evening with bittersweet news. According to Panditji, the ninth phase of the moon in the month of Maagh (December) was an auspicious day for Narayani's *Muklawa*.

Narayani beamed, knowing that only a month later she would reunite with her love. At the same time, she felt an excruciating pain in her heart. Leaving her parents behind was going to be painful.

'Isn't it strange, Juggli, that no matter where I go, my heart will always long for my loved ones? Before, I longed for Tandhan, and now I will long for my parents, you, and this whole village. Wouldn't it be better if baba and maa could live next door?' She confided in her old friend.

Juggli nodded.

'I will go and tell maa to migrate to Jhunjhunu. I am sure baba will agree. He has to go there for business often anyway.'

Narayani put forward the proposal to her mother. Ganga smiled and sat her down.

'For a girl to form her new abode, she must let go of her previous one. Only then can she fully accept and adjust to her new house and family. And parents too need to let go of their blind love for their children or else it can turn toxic. We will always be there in your heart and you, my child, in ours. For you to accept your in-laws as parents, the proximity between us must reduce, only then will you be able to make space for new changes and people.'

She kissed Narayani on her forehead. 'Every corner of this house will forever retain your presence. Your baba and I will live the rest of our lives with these memories. Besides, it's not like you can never come back. And knowing your baba, he will surely keep visiting you with one excuse or another. Now go and begin packing!'

Jhunjhunu

At dinner, Jaliram shared with the family Gurshamal's message about Narayani's *Muklawa*. He asked Tandhan to start preparations to travel to Dokwa to escort Narayani home.

'I will go along', said Ranaji, 'I won't let him travel alone. We are constantly being followed by Jhadchand's men, I am quite sure.'

'Ranaji, it's your paranoia and nothing else. The matter is old and buried now. I haven't sensed anything ill until now. Take it easy, nothing will happen', said Jaliram.

'Better safe than sorry. I will travel along with infantry. No discussions!' Ranaji said with a sense of finality.

He selected a platoon of soldiers and horsemen for their trip to Dokwa.

'You are right in taking along guards', the Nawab agreed. 'Although Hisar is a closed chapter, the hills of Devsar that fall on the way are known for dacoits. The hills aid in hiding and conducting surprise attacks. They not only rob travellers but often kill them too. Remember to start early in the morning and return before sunset.'

Although thrilled to see her daughter-in-law after months, Yamuna's heart felt restless for the safety of Tandhan. As she lifted the *thali* to apply vermillion on his forehead, it slipped from her hand and the vermillion splashed all over the floor. Ranaji dismissed what was considered to be a bad omen. 'I won't let anything bad happen.'

Dokwa

Narayani ran her palms all over the walls of the house as if feeling the grains in them and speaking to them.

'Laado, what are you doing, *bitiya?*' Gurshamal asked.

'Baba, I am feeling the whole house. I will leave in a few days...so I wanted to say goodbye and thank every little thing that has been a part of my life until now.' She took a deep, audible breath. 'Lila *tai* has invited us for dinner today. Tomorrow, Masterji has invited us for lunch. Everyone has loved me so much all these years. Will they do so once I leave? Will they even remember me, baba?' Tears filled her eyes as she spoke.

'You can never be forgotten, my child. Even if you are out of sight, you will always dwell in our hearts. Now go and get ready.' Gurshamal turned to hide his tears.

Lila kept tutoring Narayani in the dos and don'ts of a daughter-in-law and wife's role.

'Ofo, maa! Must you keep lecturing us day and night? Our ears tire and heads hurt listening.'

Masterji gifted Narayani his Bhagavad Gita wrapped in a red loincloth.

'This is your most prized possession, Masterji! You never allow anyone to touch it', said Narayani, holding it with care and reverence.

'My eyesight is getting blurry and my bones are getting weak. Thus, I am passing it on to the worthiest pair of hands I have had the privilege of teaching. Just like you did here, spread the light of your knowledge there too. Keep it and use it well, my child.'

The entire village gathered to receive Tandhan, their new son-in-law. Gurshamal's heart swelled with pride when he saw Tandhan seated on Pavan. His strength and sensitivity made him an ideal man for his daughter.

Tandhan got down and touched Ganga and Gurshamal's feet. Ganga circled her palms over his head and pressed them to her temples.

'Welcome, beta! Whenever I see you, my fear and anxiety about Laado leaving our house vanish. Your presence is very reassuring, beta. May Lord Vishnu always bless you!' Ganga said with a smile on her lips and a tear in her eyes.

Tandhan noticed the painted courtyard and his eyes went straight to the door of Narayani's room, eager to get a glimpse of his beloved wife. Unable to spot her and annoyed that she did not even come to receive him, he kept looking around, greeting everyone with a forced smile.

'Where is Narayani? I can't see her, is she not home?' Unable to hold back any more, he finally inquired.

Ranjit smiled. 'She has locked herself in her room. She does that when she is upset...'

'Upset? Let me go and speak to her.' Tandhan stood outside the room and waited until everyone left. He then knocked on the door. 'Narayani, can I join you? Even I am upset. Please open the door.'

Face smeared with tears and hair dishevelled, she opened the door. 'Why are you upset? You don't have to leave your parents.'

Even in her unkempt avatar, she appeared beautiful to him. He took a step forward and held her hand. 'Humph! So that's the matter. I would be sad too if I was in your place. So what do we—'

'I am not coming with you. I won't leave my maa and baba.' Hiding her face in her hands, she started sobbing. Holding her wrists, he parted her hands and wiped her face of the tears.

'Ok then! I will stay here with you. I will become a *ghar jamai*. Is that ok?'

She smiled. 'Why will you do that? Won't you miss

your parents and brother then?'

He turned his back to her.

'Yes, I will. But we all have to grow up and raise our own families and for that, we have to change homes. So I will do it, I am a grown man!'

She turned him around. 'I am strong and grown up too. I will dress up and be ready in a while.'

He let out a laugh and held her face in his hands. 'Yes, yes! My beautiful strong wife! Remember one thing, I love you a lot, and I love your smile, not your tears. I will bring you to Dokwa to meet your parents whenever you wish. Now smile!'

The villagers pampered Tandhan with food and gifts. They surrounded him till late at night, sharing Narayani's childhood stories and asking questions about Jhunjhunu and Hisar.

'Let's sleep now, we have to leave early in the morning', said Ranaji.

Placing pots of water next to the charpoy for them, Gurshamal spoke, 'Why don't you stay for another day, Jamaiji? Give us some more time to serve you.'

'You have already pampered us so much. Keep some for next time. Besides, work awaits back home', Tandhan answered, holding his hands.

Ganga and Gurshamal could not sleep that night. They kept looking at Narayani's face as she slept next to them, one last time. They felt a void in them widening by the minute. In a few hours, the house would be empty. Ganga blew her nose in her *odhani*.

'What will I do now? Who will I speak to? These walls and the empty house will haunt me. Even I will join you on your trade trips to Jhunjhunu.'

Gurshamal nodded, tears rolling down his cheeks.

The next morning, the convoy was ready. As Narayani sat in the *doli*, Ranaji hugged Gurshamal.

'*Bhaaya*, I can feel your pain...I can assure you of one thing though. Jaliram is a very good man and Tandhan is a remarkable boy. Your daughter will always be happy.'

Radha and Sheila had made a doll for Narayani that they gave her after holding her in a tight embrace. Narayani clutched Ganga tight. 'Maa, let me get down, I don't want to go!'

Lila pulled Ganga away and wiped Narayani's tears. Gurshamal ran a quick hand over her head and turned away as he broke down.

CHAPTER 21
A Battle

'Jai Bhavani! Hail Lord Vishnu!'

The convoy began their journey from Dokwa to Jhunjhunu.

In a few hours, they crossed the plains. Narayani watched the hills covered in little shrubs with amusement. She requested Tandhan to halt for a while, to look around and climb the hills. She had never seen hills like these before. More than happy to please his wife, Tandhan proposed a halt.

'These hills are going to be there for a long stretch, let's stop at lunch', said Ranaji.

Tandhan dismounted his horse and walked beside Narayani's doli.

'How long will it take to reach home? I am getting bored in this *doli*. Can I walk with you and enjoy some fresh air?' She asked.

He smiled and nodded. The two started walking together.

'She is a new bride! Why make her walk on this rocky path?' Ranaji said, clearly annoyed.

Narayani quickly climbed back into the *doli*. As she pulled the curtains, her eyes fell on some nearby bushes that moved unnaturally. She saw in them a pair of eyes that quickly vanished. Ignoring them, she rested for a while.

The sun was now exactly overhead and the men and horses, tired from the journey, needed a water break. Ranaji spotted a small flag over a four-stoned temple with just a *trishul* inside. Convinced that it was a safe place, he ordered the convoy to halt. Narayani pulled her *odhani* and went inside the bushes to relieve herself. As she returned, she felt as though she was being watched. Dismissing the thought yet again, she paused to take in the beauty of the surrounding hills. She climbed a big rock to get a better view. Tandhan followed.

'Don't go far!' Ranaji warned.

'You seem to love rocks and hills', said Tandhan.

She removed her veil and stretched her hands wide, letting the breeze comb through her hair. She turned around and stretched Tandhan's hands.

'We are flying! I feel on top of the world with you.'

Tandhan took her in his arms. 'I feel so too!'

'Let's move!' Ranaji ordered.

Narayani sulked as she did not want to go. Pulling down the *odhani,* she obediently climbed into the *doli*.

'The next stretch is a little dangerous. Move quickly and silently. Narayani, keep the curtains drawn. Tandhan, we will both ride beside Narayani's *doli*.'

As the surrounding hills began to converge, the path shrunk into a narrow stretch. The party crossed it at a tremendous pace and reached a point where the path began to widen yet again and opened eventually into a vast plain surrounded by hills. Relieved and now at ease after having crossed the most treacherous portion of their journey, they stopped for a water break.

The men put down the *doli* and picked up a pot of water. Taking turns, they refreshed themselves by sprinkling the water on their faces and taking a sip or two of it. While Tandhan relieved himself in the nearby bushes, Ranaji made the horses drink water.

Suddenly, the air grew thick with dust. Through the haze reverberated the sound of two dozen horses galloping towards the party.

'*Allah-hu Akbar!*' A menacing chorus pierced the air.

Everyone at the party drew their weapons, alert, blood pumping with unprecedented fervour in their veins. Tandhan and Ranaji rushed towards Narayani's *doli*.

'No matter what, do not step out. Stay still and hidden away from their view.'

A spear came flying from a distant bush and pierced one of the four men who had carried the *doli*. He fell to the ground face first, never to rise again.

'But I can…'

Two dozen horsemen and fifteen soldiers were on a brutal killing spree. The air filled with blood-curdling screams.

'This is no *akhara*, we are under attack. These are barbarians who only know how to kill. Stay inside!' Ranaji ordered, the vein in his forehead throbbing.

Dropping the curtains of Narayani's *doli*, he ran towards the enemy along with Tandhan, their swords drawn. Both mounted their horses swiftly.

'They are Jhadchand's men. I know their warfare techniques', said Ranaji. 'You defend, I will attack from behind, that's the only way to tackle them. Although they outnumber us, we can beat them. Let's finish them all. *Jai Bhavani!*'

'*Jai Bhavani!*' Tandhan yelled.

Together, the two charged forward.

Soldiers of Jhunjhunu were known for their remarkable attack skills. Narayani sat clutching her red *ghaghra*, listening attentively. She could hear swords clanging and the moans of people dying.

'*Jai Bhavani!*'

'*Allah-hu Akbar!*'

Narayani parted the curtains and peeped outside. Tandhan and Ranaji were tearing into their opponents like a force of nature. The enemies' numbers had already been halved. Seeing Ranaji and Tandhan safe, Narayani's worries eased.

Suddenly, a hand reached into the *doli* and tried to grab her. Narayani squeezed into the other corner, away from the enemy's hands. Just then, the hand retracted with a scream and a loud thud.

'Narayani!'

Narayani parted the curtain and looked outside. Tandhan sat on his horse, the blade of his sword shining bright red. 'Are you ok?'

Narayani nodded. As Tandhan galloped away, she started reciting Lord Vishnu's name.

After nearly half an hour, the sounds of swords and men reduced.

'Just two more left', cried Ranaji, 'finish them, Tandhan!'

'Jai Bhavani!' Tandhan yelled as he pushed a sword into a soldier's abdomen.

At the same time, Ranaji killed the last soldier.

'Jai Bhavani!' Tandhan and Ranaji raised their swords and yelled in unison.

'Aah!' Tandhan screamed as a spear brushed past his arm, taking a huge chunk of his flesh.

Tandhan and Ranaji turned to spot the assailant and watched in horror as twenty-odd horsemen appeared on the horizon followed by Jhadchand on an elephant. Everyone watched in shock; for a moment, it seemed that it was all over.

'We demolished the first army, we will destroy this one too! Charge! Fight!' Tandhan shouted.

'Jai Bhavani!' Ranaji cried.

'JAI BHAVANI!'

Jhadchand looked down on them with a sardonic smile. 'Tandhan', he spoke, 'call all your gods! Let's see who saves you from my vengeance today. I haven't slept peacefully in a long time. Today I will do that after killing you and taking your wife with me to serve my daughter-in-law as a maid.'

Ignoring his words, Tandhan started tearing into Jhadchand's army one soldier at a time. Jhadchand grew restless watching Tandhan as within minutes, he killed two of his men.

Meanwhile, Ranaji was fighting off five men at once. His horse fell, fractured by a powerful blow delivered by one of Jhadchand's men, so Ranaji was now on foot tackling two horsemen and three soldiers. Although unable to stop him, they had managed to push him far away from Tandhan.

By now, only five of Tandhan and Ranaji's men remained. Jhadchand looked at Ranaji, who was growing tired by the minute; his men would kill him soon. Jhadchand then looked at Tandhan. He was unstoppable, rapidly killing his remaining men. Jhadchand looked on worried; more than half of his soldiers were dead. Tandhan was in a duel with one of his finest swordsmen and the latter appeared to be on the verge of certain defeat. Jhadchand knew he had to do something.

He drew his sword and stationed his elephant next to the two of them as they fought. Just when Tandhan came into his vicinity, Jhadchand jumped down from the elephant with the sword in his hand. His knees buckled as his feet touched the ground. Steadying himself, he swung his sword at Tandhan's neck. His head went flying and landed with a soft thud on the ground. His decapitated body shook for a brief moment before collapsing.

Ranaji killed the last of the five men he had been fighting off for nearly half an hour and ran towards Jhadchand. 'You swine! How dare you? HOW DARE YOU!'

One of Jhadchand's men, barely alive, pounced from behind and punched Ranaji on the head with all his fleeting strength. He fell unconscious immediately. Jhadchand let out a thunderous laugh.

A gust of wind blew, stirring the sand in the deathly silence, parting the curtains of the *doli*. Narayani saw then her husband's severed head lying in the sand. Overcome with grief and anger, she flung her hands at the *doli's* wall and broke all her red and green glass bangles. She then jumped from the *doli* and walked towards his corpse, oblivious to the many dead bodies scattered all around her. The wind swept the *odhani* off her face. She kept walking.

She knelt beside his head and watched it in a daze. Did she know him? Could it be *him*?

Laughing uproariously, Jhadchand walked towards her. Placing the tip of his blood-stained sword right beneath Narayani's chin, he raised her head so he could see her well.

'Your delicate, beautiful face softens my heart. I cannot turn you into a slave, what a waste that would be!' He laughed. 'What should I do with you then?'

Narayani kept looking at Tandhan's head, tears flowing down her cheeks, the sharp tip of Jhadchand's sword against her chin making it bleed. Jhadchand retracted his sword, making her head droop. A strong gust of wind blew yet again, this time carrying Narayani's *odhani* with it. It then teased her long, dark hair and scattered it all over her shoulders.

'Narayani, run from that monster! RUN!' Ranaji screamed, half-conscious.

Jhadchand laughed. 'Do not fear, o beautiful one, I have no intention to kill you! Your tender beauty has changed my heart. It has been a while since my last *nikah*, I will make you my bride, my most precious bride.'

Narayani raised her head for the first time and in one swift move pried the sword out of Jhadchand's relaxed grip. She stood up and waved the sword in front of him, her eyes bloodshot, her manner terrifying.

'The sword does not suit your—'

Before he could finish his sentence, Narayani swung the sword at him. He jumped but the sword left a deep gash on his right arm and it started bleeding profusely.

Jhadchand stumbled backwards. The power in her attack conveyed her experience in handling a sword. She could kill him. She *would* kill him. Jhadchand picked up Tandhan's sword from the ground. Narayani picked up his shield.

Screaming, Narayani charged at him. Her sword landed on Jhadchand's and he pushed her back. He then swung the sword at her and it landed on her shield. This time, she pushed him back. She attacked him yet again and her sword landed on his shield. Try as he may, this time, he could not push her back.

'You monster! Marriage?'

With her hair flying in the wind and eyes bulging out, she appeared anything but human.

'Try and place a finger on me and I will annihilate you! They won't even find your ashes! Death is the only answer to your sin, Jhadchand. It is in your destiny to die today at the hands of the very woman you have widowed. *Jai Bhavani!*'

Jhadchand managed to push her back but she kept attacking with quick and heavy blows. Ranaji, who had managed to stand on his feet by now, looked on in surprise as Narayani fought a man twice her size. He ran to help her but two of Jhadchand's soldiers attacked him. While he fought them off, he kept looking at Narayani. He had already lost his nephew; he would not let the same fate befall his nephew's bride.

Despite being much shorter than him, Narayani was overpowering Jhadchand. While he was losing his strength, she appeared not to tire at all. Jhadchand had underestimated her. He could not stop her alone. He called for help and two of his soldiers came running. As they engaged with Narayani, he ran and climbed his elephant and looked down in horror. She had already killed both of them and was now fighting with three more of Jhadchand's men. She appeared like Mahakali in *Rudra roop*.

'Kill her, you morons!' Jhadchand yelled.

Narayani ran towards the first horse in her sight. Just then, a soldier attacked her from behind. The blade of his sword carved a deep cut in her back and blood started gushing out. Narayani turned and in one swift motion pushed the sword into his stomach. Another soldier pulled her by the hair. Swinging her left hand, she threw him off with the shield. Jhadchand grabbed a spear and threw it at her. Narayani bent to her left but it still grazed her neck. She picked it up and threw it at the last soldier on a horse, killing him instantly. As he fell, Narayani pulled the spear from the soldier's corpse, ready to charge again.

Ranaji was still fighting the two soldiers. He could see from a distance Jhadchand seated on his elephant, fear written all over his face. All of his men were dead except the two that Ranaji was fighting. He saw Narayani, her skin as red as her clothes, her eyes raging, her manner maniacal.

'Crush her!' Jhadchand ordered the mahout.

The elephant began moving in Narayani's direction. She quickly jumped on a horse whose rider she had killed just a while ago. Riding the horse at breakneck speed, she raced towards Jhadchand's elephant. Now in Jhadchand's proximity, with the horse lead still in her hand, Narayani stood on the horse, grabbed Jhadchand's flowing attire and threw him to the ground.

'Finish him, Narayani!' Ranaji screamed.

Standing over him, Narayani raised the sword in both hands. She brought it down at lightning speed and stopped an inch away from Jhadchand's stomach.

'Get up, you rascal! I will not give you an easy death!'

She turned and walked towards Tandhan's body. Confused, Jhadchand shot up and removed his dagger. As she bent down, he charged at her with the dagger. She swung the sword in full force, cutting his head. It went flying and landed far from the decapitated body. Ranaji ran towards Narayani, now on the verge of collapsing, and held her.

'Who are you? A human or a *devi*? You are no ordinary girl, who are you?'

Without uttering a word, she freed herself from Ranaji's grip and steadied herself. She looked at Tandhan's body for a long moment, then started walking towards his head. With shivering hands, she lifted it up and brought it back to where the body lay. Then falling on her knees, she let out a howl most painful, tears flowing uninterrupted. The wind made an eerie noise, grieving for the young widow. With Tandhan's head in her lap, Narayani kept thinking of the precious few moments she had spent with her beloved. Having lost so much blood, her body struggled to stay upright. And even as her vision began to blur, she sat there grieving, for her heart pained far more than her body ridden with wounds.

Ranaji watched in silence, helpless. Only moments before she had been this force of nature, tearing apart the enemy like a ruthless killer. And now that she had avenged her beloved's death, there was nothing left to do but grieve. The battle had made Ranaji see Narayani in a new light. She was not just a *bahurani*. She was certainly no ordinary woman. She was a *Devi's* avatar.

'You personify Mata Bhavani. I was mistaken to have underestimated your power and skill. You surpass all living warriors. I am sure you are Durga in human form. Please let me escort you back home. Your wounds are serious and the sun is beginning to set.'

Narayani looked at the sun sternly, as if commanding it to slow down its journey back home. She then looked up at the vultures circling above, waiting to feast on the dead bodies.

'Gather some wood and fetch water immediately', she spoke in an authoritative tone.

Adopting a fatherly tone, Ranaji spoke, '*Bitiya*, there is no water body around here and the sun will set soon. Let's leave before it gets dark, we will return with the family tomorrow early in the morning. You need immediate medical attention. I have already lost Tandhan, I cannot afford to lose you. What will I tell Jaliram and Gurshamal ji? Please get up!'

'How can you even think that I will leave him here for the vultures or Jhadchand's people who will arrive soon? NEVER!' Her eyes spewed fire. 'Do as I say; dig! There is water two feet below.'

Assisted by one of his wounded men, Ranaji began digging. In the meantime, Narayani scoured the area for pieces of wood and twigs. Her skin layered thick with blood and sweat, as she walked around, her entire life played before her eyes. Every once in a while, she would break down...how had life turned around in the blink of an eye! She was getting weaker and weaker with every passing minute.

Ranaji kept digging, unsure if they would find water. He kept going for it was Narayani's demand, the only one she had ever made. He would glance at her occasionally as she put together a funeral pyre for her husband. The sun appeared to slow down. Narayani's tears refused to dry. Vultures started feasting on a few corpses a little further away.

Breathing heavily, suddenly, Narayani collapsed next to Tandhan's body. Ranaji rushed towards her. '*Bitiya*, don't be stubborn, let's go home, you need urgent treatment. I beg of you, my eyes have seen enough death for a lifetime already, please don't make me suffer any more.'

'Dig fast!' She screamed.

With tears in his eyes, Ranaji resumed work. A few minutes later, to their surprise, water started gushing out of the ground. They immediately filled a pot and gave it to Narayani. Dipping her *odhani* in the pot of water, she started cleaning Tandhan's body with the affection of a mother and the broken heart of a wife. She adjusted his attire and placed the *pagdi* on his head. Placing his head on her lap, she cleaned the bloodstains on his face. Her body had turned numb but not her heart.

Suddenly, she collapsed on him. Ranaji held her by the shoulder.

'*Bitiya! Bitiya!*'

She opened her eyes with a start.

'Let's go, *bitiya*! Please!'

Cupping her palms together, she filled them with water from the pot and splashed it all over her face, tied her hair, adjusted her *borolo* and covered her head with the *odhani*. She then looked up at the heavens and, with her eyes closed, offered a silent prayer.

'It is time for our departure. Please allow us to go.' She requested Ranaji.

'No! NO!'

Sobbing, Narayani joined her palms together. 'My journey is over, Ranaji. My purpose is fulfilled. I had descended to this planet to unite with my beloved and now it's time we enter the heavens together and live in peace. I have nothing to live for now, my breath and body have announced their departure; now please allow us to be together, Ranaji. I can see Lord Vishnu smiling at me, telling me to leave this earth. Tandhan and my destinies have been entwined since the birth of this universe. He kept his promise, I must keep mine. Please do not delay, Ranaji, say yes...'

Ranaji was speechless. He did not know what to say or do. She was taking her last breaths, it was evident. How could he say no to her last wish? Yet he could not gather the courage or will to do it.

'I too shall die. How will I live after seeing you both die like this?' Ranaji cried.

'You have a purpose to fulfil too, Ranaji, just like us. I bestow you with a responsibility today...to spread the word in all neighbouring towns and villages...to educate their girls, to teach them self-defence, to make them aware of their own powers and abilities so that they can fight for their honour, become self-reliant, and build a better society. Will you, Ranaji?' She spoke, her voice a mere whisper, her eyes barely open.

Wiping his tears, he nodded. He had a purpose now. He nodded the permission with streaming eyes and a heavy heart. Narayani, began rubbing her *lac chuda* to ignite the fire, mumbling the *Vishnu Sahastranaam* at the foot of the pyre, her skin now pale from having lost so much blood. The sun was now a bright orange ball, steadily dipping down. Narayani fell silent. Ranaji broke down. Strong winds began to blow. Heaven itself was abiding by Narayani's last wishes. Ranaji stood there watching the two get engulfed by the flames, his hands joined in reverence and eyes full of pain. The sun finally set.

Ranaji started walking towards his horse, his gait like a ghost. He climbed the horse and lay on it, and let it carry him wherever it wanted. In front of his closed eyes played the final moments of his beloved nephew and his wife. He recalled how Narayani had transformed into an avatar of Durga and Parvati. And then, Narayani's last words echoed in his ears. He got up, grabbed the reins of his horse and sped towards Jhunjhunu. He had a purpose, to spread Narayani's story, to fulfil her wish.

Ranaji narrated the story to everyone he met on his way. People came to the spot where the battle was fought and found huge flames erupting from Tosham hills, an active volcanic region, as if giving a rightful final farewell to those who had died.

Narayani's story spread far and wide. Her grit, conviction, and courage turned her into a Devi.

Epilogue

Ranaji finished narrating the story to a stark, resonating silence. Everyone sat still, lost in deep thoughts. The sun's final rays for the day fell on the trident, this time a rich golden yellow, and illuminated every face.

'She fought until she had nothing left in her', said a woman.

'What an extraordinary girl!' Another said.

'But she was nothing like a girl! Learnt martial arts, rode a horse, went to school…only boys do that!' A young man said dismissively.

'NO!' Ranaji said, his voice filled with rage. 'She was nothing like a boy, she was a girl who realised all her strength and potential in a very short life. She lived and died so that people like you would learn to stop treating girls like they were lesser humans. I was like you once, I thought that she was a very ill-mannered girl because she went to school and had a mind of her own…'

'But she was!' The young man replied.

'Fool! I saw her fight that monster Jhadchand like

a goddess…I couldn't do what she did, even you and ten other men like you together couldn't fight like she did. Until then, I thought she was just an ordinary girl, emboldened by a father keen to ruin our culture. But when I saw her take charge the way she did, I realised, at that moment, my folly…how stupid of us all to think that our culture is to bind a woman with superficial ties…to expect her to only cook, clean, and give birth when she can do and be so much more!'

'Ranaji', said the little girl, 'so I can play with a bat and ball too? Like my brother?'

'You can do anything, my child.'

'And what if I want to grow up and become the Sarpanch?'

'You can do whatever you want.'

A wave of murmur ran through the group.

'But Ranaji…she was a goddess; rules that bind human beings did not apply to her', said a woman.

'Her life is proof that rules set by people like you and me mean nothing. Within every girl is a goddess, and our rules do nothing but hold them back. Set your daughters free, let them live, let them make their own decisions. Strong, independent women build strong societies. If you worship Narayani yet treat your own mothers, daughters, and sisters with disrespect, it is all futile. To worship Narayani, give the women in your life respect, love and, most importantly, freedom.'

'To worship Narayani, we must worship her values', said the young man.

Ranaji nodded, his mouth breaking into a smile at last.

'Ranaji, I found all my answers', said the little girl, 'and I understand now how to become self-reliant and walk on the path of righteousness to create a better world. I feel strong now, Ranaji.'

'WE ALL DO!'

Every heart felt a wave of calm and strength wash over it, content at last that their visit to Shakti Dham had given them everything they wanted.

One by one, they started walking out. Ranaji, his head now resting on the pole of the trident, kept looking long after everyone left, ruminating over Narayani's story. She had kept her promise. And so had he.

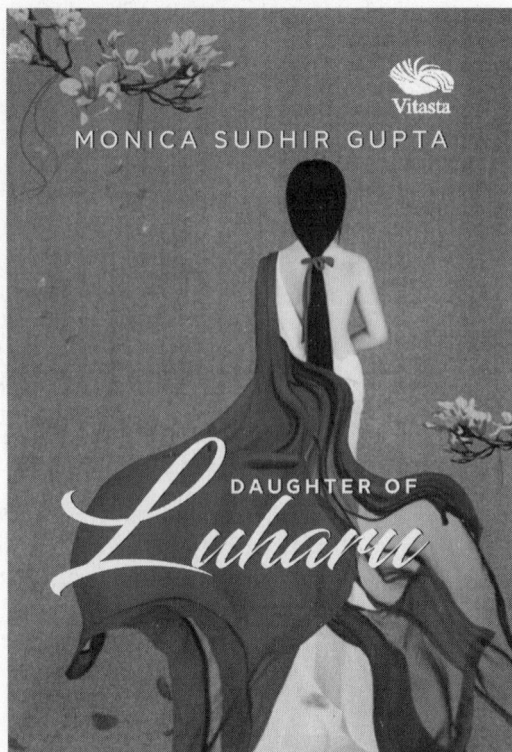

Daughter of Luharu

by Monica Sudhir Gupta (Author)

4.9 ★★★★★ ⌄   31 ratings

Kusum Choppra

★★★★★ **MUST READ!!!!**
Reviewed in India on 26 February 2022
Verified Purchase

Daughter of Luharu" by Monica S Gupta is a poignant reminder of an era being pushed out of memory...

Ujaala Lal

★★★★★ **An amazing read**
Reviewed in India on 6 May 2022
Verified Purchase

It is not a story of a woman but the life of every woman who survived partition...

Anitha PN

★★★★★ **A riveting page turner.**
Reviewed in India on 23 March 2022
Verified Purchase

A riveting page turner that chronicles the life o woman and her travails...

Aryaman Gupta

★★★★★ **It's like watching a movie ...**
Reviewed in India on 20 February 2022
Verified Purchase

The writing is fabulous and if you are from the northern part of India I am sure it would get yc imagination running. It's like you are not readir the book but watching a movie. Fabulous work